# DEAD LEAVES

## KEALAN PATRICK BURKE

Dead Leaves
9 Tales from the Witching Season
Kealan Patrick Burke

Print Edition

*Dead Leaves* copyright © 2018 by Kealan Patrick Burke

Visit the author at www.kealanpatrickburke.com

# CONTENTS

INTRODUCTION ................................................................................1

ANDROMEDA ....................................................................................3

SOMEONE TO CARVE THE PUMPKINS ...........................................23

HAVEN ............................................................................................29

HOW THE NIGHT RECEIVES THEM ................................................43

TONIGHT THE MOON IS OURS .......................................................49

THE TOLL ........................................................................................65

WILL YOU TELL THEM I DIED QUIETLY? .......................................77

THE TRADITION .............................................................................87

THE ONE NIGHT OF THE YEAR ......................................................97

RECOMMENDED BOOKS ...............................................................105

RECOMMENDED MOVIES ..............................................................111

ABOUT THE AUTHOR ....................................................................119

# DEAD LEAVES

## Kealan Patrick Burke

# INTRODUCTION

IT'S OCTOBER 3ᴿᴰ AS I WRITE THIS, and hotter than it has any business being. The sun is shining, although with that burnished antique quality of light unique to autumn, and it's quiet except for the sound of dead leaves falling from the trees that surround my house. My neighbors have started decorating their houses with the expected fare: plastic skeletons, corn dollies, fake cobwebs, and pumpkins. Some of them keep it simple, others go all out, festooning their homes with an abandon usually reserved for Christmas. These houses are positively shrouded in cobwebs, amber lights, dangling bats and witches; the yards are full of foam gravestones, zombies frozen in the act of emerging from their plots, malevolent scarecrows, and bubbling cauldrons; and their porches are a veritable gallery of plastic ghouls and hangmen.

It brings a smile to my face to see these people, from the painfully straitlaced to the inordinately ebullient, united in their guilty excitement for Halloween. Because that's really what it's all about, isn't it? Fun. We enjoy being scared, and we enjoy scaring. No matter how reserved or serious our lives might have become in the long dark hallway of years that separate us from our childhoods, Halloween remains that one time of the year in which the masks of our adulthood are not only permitted, but encouraged to come off, replaced by whatever terrible, transient visage with which we choose to replace them. For one night, we get to retreat from the world of adult responsibility and enjoy being the monsters. We get to dress up, give out candy, bay at the moon, or huddle up on the couch with our nearest and dearest while taking mutual comfort in the fact that the noise we just heard outside was probably just the wind, that the vampires and werewolves and masked killers on the TV are restricted to the world of fantasy. That we're safe. It's a naïve state of mind we subconsciously carry with us all year round.

We're safe.

Nothing can harm us. The world, despite its horrors, exists beyond the borders of our town, and nothing bad ever happens here. But, of course it does, and on Halloween, we invite the monsters in, permit them their one night to terrorize us before slinking back to their graves and crypts.

Halloween is controllable horror. We allow the monsters their time in the moonlight until we send them away. We watch scary films on TV, but can change the channel and switch it off whenever we like. We read the books but can close them if it gets to be too much.

We control it.

It's a safe kind of scary.

And considering how hostile it seems our world has become, where urban legends of yesteryear become ideas for the unstable, where no child walks alone after dark, and no door or window goes unlocked, it's nice to have that kind of control.

Halloween provides us with the choice to be scared, or to scare others. It allows us to vicariously slip behind the mask and see the world through the eyes of things that evoke fear in others. It allows us to be scared out of our wits, safe in the knowledge that it isn't real.

For one night, and one night only, we're the monsters.

This is horror, ladies and gentlemen. In books, movies, videogames, horror is escapism no more or less than Halloween. We wear the masks for a short time, knowing they can always be removed. We get to be scared in a safe environment, and nobody gets hurt.

This is Halloween.

This is Horror.

Celebrate it.

– Kealan Patrick Burke

# ANDROMEDA

**H**OW DO I LOOK?" MOM ASKS.

It's an unnecessary question, so Hannah doesn't bother checking to be sure her answer is the accurate one. Her mother doesn't always look her best, especially on those nights in which she seeks solace from her loneliness in a bottle of expensive wine, but today, like every weekday, she's in work mode, glammed up and ready to make richer people than her buy property they probably don't really want or need.

"Amazing."

"That'd mean more to me if you actually looked at me when you said it."

Hannah shrugs in response. Her eyes are fixed on her phone, more specifically the details of the boy who just followed her on Instagram. He's cute, but has few followers and little personal information, so while Mom frets about her appearance, Hannah tries to deduce whether or not this "Paul M." is legit or just another spambot.

"Did you have breakfast, honey?"

"Yeah."

"Something nutritious no doubt."

"A Pop-Tart."

"Great." Mom scoops up her keys from the counter. "Do me a favor and grab an apple or something when you head out."

"Yep."

The sigh tells Hannah what's coming. She doesn't brace herself, doesn't need to. She's heard this same old line a thousand times before.

"Honey, you really need to start weaning yourself off that phone. I can hardly tell what your face looks like anymore."

Hannah lowers the phone and offers her a pained grin. "Still there, still unremarkable."

"Oh baby, don't say that. You're beautiful."

"Sure. Like you're allowed to say anything different."

"Stop that. I mean it. You're gorgeous. And your skin will clear up in no time now that you're using that...what is it?" And here comes the forced maternal reassurance. Hannah returns the iPhone to its ever-present spot in front of her face to thwart the unwanted contact—the cheek-pinching, the hair-tucking, the chin-raising—and is relieved when the strategy proves successful. Her mother stops a few feet away and folds her arms, Hannah only aware of her as a fuzzy image in her periphery.

"Thanks, Mom. Really." She returns her focus to the dark-haired, dark-skinned boy with the pierced eyebrows, tattoos, and apparent penchant for crazy colorful art. And the abs...*Good God, please let him be real.* She taps the heart icon on the shirtless picture.

"I just worry about you. I mean, I'm all for you kids and your phones, but don't you think you might be...I don't know, depending on it a bit much. I feel like I never see you without it."

"Why would I be without it? A lot of my friends are on here. It's how we stay in touch. It's how everyone stays in touch. And you were the one who bought me the phone, if I remember correctly, for that specific reason, so I could *make* some friends, right? Wasn't that the point?"

"Yes, but *real* friends, honey. People you hang out with."

"I hang out with them all the time."

"In real life?"

"Define real life."

"In person."

"I see plenty of them in person." Not strictly true, but Mom doesn't need to know that.

"Tonight, for instance. It's Halloween. Do you have plans?"

"Like what?"

"Like, anything?"

Hannah shrugs. In the time it took her mother to voice her concerns, she hearted ten of Paul M.'s pictures, which she meant as a clear expression of interest, but now she worries it might appear creepy. Like, *who is this chick stalking all my pix* kinda creepy. She decides it's better to exercise moderation and un–likes half of them. That done, she texts Fiona, her thumbs tapping a soft beat across the virtual keyboard.

*Wanna hang out tonight? Mom's busting my balls.*

Two seconds later, the response: *Fo shizzle.*

"Hannah?"

"Yes, Mom, I do have plans. I'm going over to Fiona's to watch movies and hand out candy."

"Is Max going to be there?"

A withering look over the top of the phone. "Really? 'Go out, Hannah. Make friends, Hannah. Get off the Internet and start socializing, Hannah.' But now it's: 'who's going to be there?'"

"I don't think it's an unreasonable question considering he's six years older than you and known for being a bit of a rough sort."

"Max is doing better. He's got a job and everything."

"Still, I'm not sure how I feel about you hanging around him. He's trouble."

"I'm going to hang out with Fiona, not her brother. I don't even know if he's going to be there, and if he is, you know he just hangs out in his room by himself doing whatever."

"Doing whatever. That's reassuring."

On the Internet, a news story is doing the rounds. Hannah is hardly comforted to see that for once it's not about white cops shooting black people or Trump's latest attempt to rile up the country. Instead, it looks like an article about some kind of anomaly in the Baltic Sea. As a UFO enthusiast, she bookmarks the article to read later.

"Mom. Max's not a problem. You're making it one."

"His *behavior* makes it one."

"He's never tried anything with me. He just has some issues. It's town gossip that made him the villain."

"Sounds like the naïve testimony of a future victim."

"So—what? Want me to cancel? Because I can if it'll make you feel better."

Mom shakes her head, conceding defeat. "No, go. I don't want to be *that* parent."

Just then, her mother's eyes catch and trap the sunlight through the kitchen window and Hannah can't help but smile. Her mother really is a very pretty woman, even if she spends way too much time doubting that fact, a preoccupation that will inevitably lead her to overcompensate, if the brochures and information pamphlets from notable plastic surgeons on her mother's nightstand are any indication. She doesn't need work done, of course, but her vanity, made worse by the loss of a husband to a much younger woman, will trump all arguments to the contrary.

Hannah's appraisal doesn't go unnoticed, and has the desired effect of changing the subject, for which she is grateful. Her mother smiles questioningly. "What's that look for?"

"You look hot, Mom. I mean, Cate Blanchett hot." A slight exaggeration, but it won't be the first time Laura Goldman has drawn such a comparison, which makes it the perfect one to employ.

"You think so?"

"Hell, yeah."

Clearly pleased, Mom gives a little wiggle. "Well, thank you, honey."

"De nada." Back to the world contained within her phone. It's time to stop obsessing over the legitimacy of Abs Boy and possible UFOs. A few taps of a finger and she's on Snapchat.

"Shit, well, I'd better get moving," Mom says. "Say a prayer that today's the day I finally unload that three-bedroom over on Sancus."

"That the one with the bidet?"

"The very same."

Hannah chuckles. "*Bidet.* Maybe you'll get someone who's anal-retentive."

A groan. "See you later. What is it you girls say? *I'm out.*"

"Something like that, but it sounds weird coming from you."

"Later, then," Mom says with a grin, and is gone on a swirling wave of expensive perfume.

With a shake of her head, Hannah flips through the pictures and videos of people she hardly knows, breaking from the hypnotic stream only when two text messages ding in quick succession. The first is from Fiona, arguably her only friend not confined to the phone: *Running late. B there in a few.*

The second is from a number she doesn't know. It happens more often than she likes, a consequence of using a number that belonged to someone else before she acquired it. Sometimes she gets voice mails from debt collectors looking for a Leroy Downes. Other times, texts from jilted lovers who have no idea their heartfelt pleas are being received and read by a stranger. Rather than preoccupy herself with their dilemma, Hannah always deletes the texts and blocks the numbers, but apparently Leon's a bit of a player, and so she still occasionally hears from another of his broken hearts.

This one reads: *Keep looking at your phone.*

A weird message for sure, but then many of them are, and so she blocks the number and deletes the text. Sooner or later, 'ol Bad Bad Leroy Downes is going to run out of conquests, surely, unless the number was never his and he intentionally gave it to his one-night stands so he'd never have to hear from them. A number which just happens to be Hannah's. With a sigh, she sets down her phone and goes to grab her backpack.

The screen on her iPhone flickers.

* * *

The route to school is short enough to walk, but ever since Fiona got her provisional license, it's far cooler to drive, especially since she has the use of her brother's Camaro while he's deployed. Not that he's aware of this, of course. If he was, he'd go AWOL just long enough to put her in hospital, because after his country, women, and the Buckeyes, the 1971 Camaro SS is his pride and joy. It's a classic car, though Fiona only cares that it looks badass and gets ample attention from the kinds of guys she envisions herself dating, even if that's unlikely. Like Hannah, she is what kinder folk would term homely and crueler folk would call a geek, and though progressive modern attitudes might condemn such labels, at Hayes High School, negative profiling is still practiced with abandon.

"He's pretty hot," Fiona says as she carefully guides her brother's obsession out into traffic.

Hannah nods and scrolls through more pictures of Paul M. "Doesn't say where he's from though."

"Not our school, that's for sure. We'd have noticed him."

"For sure," Hannah mumbles. "Hey, is Max going to be—?"

A sudden deafening wail and Fiona yanks the wheel hard to the right. "*Jesus!*"

Startled, Hannah jumps, the panic rising as Fiona swerves into the bicycle lane to avoid getting clipped by a police cruiser as it blasts by, sirens blazing. "Why didn't you pull over?" she asks, heart pounding in her chest.

"I just did, dummy."

"I mean when you heard the siren."

"I *didn't* hear it until it was on top of me. Did you?"

"No. You scared the hell out of me."

"Yeah, me too. It came out of nowhere."

She pulls the car to a halt at the curb. Two ambulances and another police cruiser wail by the Camaro, matching the pace of their colleague.

"Must be an accident," Hannah muses.

"Yeah, well, there'd have been an accident waiting for me at home if that cop had knocked my mirror off."

They're parked beneath the gently shifting shade of an elm tree on a quiet neighborhood street. Every stoop save one is dressed for the season: grinning pumpkins, cartoonish witches, sheeted ghosts, and plastic tombstones. In one yard, an elderly man gently dabs crimson paint onto the mouth of the six-foot polystyrene zombie he has propped up in the middle of his lawn. In another, a mother and her two young children are stuffing with hay the sleeves of a recumbent scarecrow. In a third, a man in a business suit stands staring across the lawns at both the mother and her kids and the old man. To Hannah, it looks as if behind his spectacles he is weeping, though she can't be sure it isn't just the light.

After what seems like hours, the traffic starts to move.

"Finally. Mr. Douglas is going to have our asses," Fiona grumbles. "'I can hear that old fart now: 'Less than a mile from school and you still can't make it on time, Ms. Kelly'."

"He's the worst."

As they pull away from the curb, Hannah casts a final look back at the man in the suit. As if sensing her attention, he turns his head in her direction, his spectacles flashing in the October sunlight, making burning white holes of his eyes. He smiles, raises his right arm, and jams his fist into his mouth.

* * *

In Mrs. Lethem's History class, hands beneath her desk so that she won't be seen texting, Hannah writes: *dis day iz draggn.*

A moment later, the phone hums to indicate Fiona's reply: *rite? Called it abt Douglas. gv me d usual shit. also hd sum red crusty stuff in d corners of his mouth. Ketchup, prob. couldn't stop lookn at it. almost barfed.*

Hannah: *LOL.*

"Ms. Goldman? I know that's not your phone you're messing with."

Expertly pocketing the cell, Hannah clasps her hands atop her textbook and mimics focus. "No, Miss."

"Good," Mrs. Lethem says, on her face a familiar look of warning. Last time she caught Hannah using her phone in class, she'd confiscated it for the rest of the day. Hannah didn't think it would bother her all that much, but she'd ended up feeling like a drug addict forced to go cold turkey— unmoored, unanchored, lost, and even as she'd told herself she was being ridiculous, her hands began to shake at the behest of offended nerves. That day she had learned what it must be like for heavy smokers to go without cigarettes for even a short time. She hadn't known what to do with her hands; her chest had started to hurt. Then, the unreasonable, paranoid thoughts about what she might be missing online, and what might be *said* about her in her absence. Preposterous, ridiculous notions which nevertheless stuck like kernels of popcorn between her teeth. When at last Mrs. Lethem returned her phone, it took everything in her not to weep with relief. Since then she has exercised a reasonable measure of caution, though the further she gets from that dark day, the easier it is to forget just how bad it really was. She tells herself that if it happened now she would handle it better, and yet at her teacher's summons, she is quick to stash the phone because the simple truth is that she doesn't like to be without it. Ever. It's a window and through it the world looks better, less complicated, more controllable, and it seems whenever she's forced to look up from it, it's to look into the eyes of someone who can't hope to understand her the way online people do.

As Mrs. Lethem drones on about things that could just as easily be googled, Hannah puts her face in her hands and looks out the window. The view of the high school grounds, from the stretch of grass to the chain-link fence bordering the street, reminds her of that scene in the old version of the movie *Halloween* when Jamie Lee Curtis is in class and sees the serial killer Michael Myers watching her from his car. There is no masked madman watching Hannah on this Hallows Eve, however, nothing so interesting, just longhaired Mr. Murphy, the groundskeeper, raking up the dead leaves, and as usual, looking none too thrilled about it.

"Ms. Goldman, that's the second time today I've had to fight for your attention."

Hannah winces and looks back at the teacher. "Sorry."

"There won't be a third, understand?"

"Yes."

Mrs. Lethem looks pale, tired, her dark eyes darker than usual, as if she might snap at any second, so Hannah decides not to press her luck and fakes attentiveness until, an eternity later, the electronic bell chimes the end of the charade.

As she gathers her books, her attention is drawn once more to the window, where Mr. Murphy is standing stock-still and staring at the back of his hands, as if it's the first time he's ever seen them, an impression aided by the confusion on his face. The rake lies buried amid a pile of red, orange, and yellow leaves, forgotten.

Beyond the fence, more sirens fill the air.

* * *

With only five minutes before Math class, Hannah hurries into the bathroom to meet Fiona, who she finds leaning against the sinks, arms folded, and staring at one of the closed stall doors.

"What's up?" Hannah asks, palming her phone and checking for messages.

"Listen."

She does, and hears nothing.

"What is it I'm supposed to be—?"

"*Listen.*"

Again, she does, and again, detects no sound from the stall. In a whisper: "Is somebody taking a particularly interesting dump? C'mon, Fi, help me out here."

A look of confusion uncannily similar to the one she saw on the face of the groundskeeper passes over her friend's face, but then is just as quickly gone. Fiona shrugs and turns to inspect her reflection as she washes her hands. "I don't know. Thought someone was crying in there."

"What's unusual about that?" Given the high rate of breakups and fakeups among the students, finding someone crying in the bathroom is hardly a notable event.

Another shrug as Fi soaps up her hands. "Nothing I guess. You want to hit Arby's for lunch?"

"Sure."

"Can you buy? Spent all my money on gas."

"No problem."

Hannah checks her phone, relieved to be out of the line of sight of the people opposed to such things, and it seems with each passing day there are even more of them. Text-Nazis, she calls them, a group so prevalent inside and outside the halls of education, that she looks forward to living on her own where if she wants to just stay in bed all day glued to her phone, she can do so without judgment.

"Ugh, my eyebrows look like shit," Fiona remarks, but Hannah isn't listening. With limited time before class resumes, she's forced to speed-check her various social media accounts (Facebook, Twitter, Instagram, and Snapchat.) But what she sees on Instagram stays her scrolling thumb.

"Hey, Fi."

"Hmm?"

"What do you make of this?"

Fiona breaks away from her reflection to squint at Hannah's screen. After a moment's inspection, she rolls her eyes. "He's a weirdo, that's what I make of it."

"Yeah, but...it wasn't like this earlier."

"So, he changed them. So what?"

"Hang on a sec." Hannah taps each picture in turn, starting with the most recent. "No, the dates show these pictures have been here since..." Tap, tap, tap. "Since the beginning of the year."

"And?"

"And there were different pictures there this morning. How did he change them all and not have the dates reflect that? If he posted them all within the past few hours, then that's what the dates should say, right? But according to this, these pictures have been here for months."

Fiona produces from her purse an eyebrow pencil and leans in closer to the mirror. "God, don't freak out about it. You don't even know the guy, or what his Instagram looks like on a normal day. Maybe this is a trick he likes to pull every now and then. Unfollow and move on, babe."

Hannah supposes her friend is right. She doesn't know anything about the mysterious Paul M and his sexy tattooed abs, but it would have been nice if he'd been legit, and by legit she realizes she means *legitimately interested*, which is a futile hope. Adding her on Instagram was hardly a definitive expression of romantic interest. In a way, replacing his drool-worthy pictures with dozens upon dozens of close-up shots of his hands only helps her avoid the comedown later when she wakes to find that he's inevitably unfollowed her first. That is, after all, how it usually goes. The good-looking guys add her to pump up their follower numbers. Most of them never even know what she looks like.

"Maybe he's an artist," Fiona says. "Maybe it's some kind of an art-thing."

Hannah swaps Instagram for Facebook. "Yeah, maybe." She turns toward the mirror just as the stall door opens behind her.

In that moment, it becomes clear that Fiona was right about the sounds she heard coming from inside the stall, because the girl who emerges looks devastated. Watching in the mirror, it takes a moment for Hannah to recognize her as Avery Thompson, the cheerleader, and naturally, one of the more popular girls in Hayes High. Her ordinarily lustrous blonde hair is a tangled mess, and her mascara is smudged around her eyes, which only serves to emphasize the chalk-like pallor of her face. Hannah's instinct is to inquire about the girl's well-being, but the gulf between their positions on the social ladder gives her pause and robs the words from her mouth, so she goes back to her phone. Fiona, however, addresses Avery via her reflection in the mirror. "You okay, girl?"

Hannah looks up in time to see two things happen at once, neither one of them easily explained.

Avery smiles, her eyes widening, giving her a manic look. "I saw the stars," she says, sounding high as a kite. "Oh, God, they were so beautiful." Then, so quickly Hannah will never be positive she saw it at all, the acoustic-tile panel over the toilet in the stall Avery just vacated *hops* as what appear to be a half dozen hands withdraws up into the ceiling.

"Did...?" Hannah starts to say, a lump in her throat. "Did you guys see that?"

"Do you need help?" Fiona asks, ignoring the question, but there is an edge to her voice that betrays her concern, and that's to be expected. On a good day, Avery Thompson would sneer at them in the hall, if she deigned to register their presence at all, so despite the girl's pitiful appearance now, it will take more than a crying jag for Fiona to genuinely care about her well-being.

"Andromeda is all hands," Avery replies, and giggles. Then her smile fades as she makes a clumsy effort to fix her hair. "We'll see them soon."

Pencil poised above her eye, Fiona watches Avery walk out of the room like a car crash victim. "And then *that* happened," she says, and scoffs. "*Lifestyles of the Rich and Brainless.*"

Hannah's eyes are on the water-stained panel in the ceiling above the toilet stall. She wants to take a closer look, sees herself standing atop the rim of the toilet bowl and poking that panel open in an effort to uncover whatever it might be hiding. Instinct tells her there's probably a bunch of horny guys up there who have taken the whole Peeping Tom thing to new levels of ingenuity, but how on earth did they fit up there, and surely the tiles wouldn't support the weight of one guy, never mind a half dozen? But then her phone dings and Fiona elbows her as she stows the pencil and zips up her purse. "C'mon, H, class is in session."

Hannah checks her messages as she follows her friend to the door.

There are two of them. The first is from her father. *Hey, just checking in. Miss you, kiddo.*

She deletes it, a burning knot of anger deep in her stomach. *Sure you do, asshole.* On the heels of this impulsive thought, she immediately feels a twinge of guilt. She loves her father, of course she does. Her truncated time with him is filled with more good memories than bad ones. That one bad one though, the worst one, is of him leaving and not looking back, and no matter how logically or fairly she looks at it, it feels like the worst kind of betrayal.

Her phone dings again.

The second is a mass text from the same unknown number as before, and like all mass texts, it garnered dozens of responses that were sent to every number on the list.

*Ding, ding, ding!*

Hannah can only watch as message after message appears in her inbox, making her phone sound like a fire station alarm. She puts it on vibrate, which only makes it slightly less annoying.

The initial message reads: *Keep your eyes on your phone. It's started. You'll be safer if you don't look.*

Hannah only has time to scan the responses before Fiona drags her bodily out of the bathroom with some muttered admonishment about addiction to social media, but what she did see was enough to unnerve her.

*They're coming out of the walls, out of us. So beautiful. Let them in. Such love. They shine.*

*Who the fuck is this? How did u get my number? Blocked.*

*Our fathers are here. It brought them home.*

*The lines, the age, the skin, the salvation. The LIGHT.*

*Wrong number, bro.*

*Please take me off this list. It's annoying.*

*The patterns, my God, do you see them? Our hands are maps of their galaxies.*

*Here's my dick, bitches. Hit me up, lol.*

*Happy Halloween, every1!*

*Road Island is gon.*

*Andromeda is calling.*

* * *

Mr. Donovan doesn't show for math class, but the expected chaos doesn't occur in his absence. Instead of the students forming their given cliques, laughing and generally doing what high schoolers do when the cage is left open, the class remains atypically subdued. A few of the more troublesome kids look around in confusion. There is some quiet conversation. A few kids use the opportunity to study or do their homework. Most consult their phones. Which is how it emerges that something has indeed been knocked off-kilter in the world. There are scattered reports of a suspected terrorist attack off the coast of Rhode Island, something about a naval vessel being sunk and explosions along the coastline. Colors under the sea. Flashing lights in the sky. The reports are confused, conflicting, unfinished. Hannah tries calling her Mom and is sent to voicemail. She doesn't worry, not yet. Her mother rarely answers the phone during the day unless it's a client. A google search of the top news stories proves no more illuminating than the scuttlebutt among her classmates. Every story differs. The only commonalities are that there has been an explosion, lights and colors, and mass injuries. *Something* has happened, but if it's really as serious as it appears, then why are they still in school? Where are the adults and the announcements? Then Hannah realizes she hasn't heard *any* announcements today, from Farris or anyone else, and when she cocks an ear toward the small speaker over the classroom door, she detects the faintest crackle, the transmitted sound of ambience from another room, as if someone is leaning on the TALK button of the PA in the principal's office.

*I should go home*, she thinks. On the desk, her phone buzzes and moves toward her like a sentient thing.

Apprehensive now, she picks it up, and breathes a sigh of relief.

It catches in her throat, almost strangling her, when she reads the message on the screen.

It's from her mom.

*Have you seen it yet, honey engine turning love? The stars, the fire, the swirling whorling patterns in our hands? We're going coming bringing us home come home there's lice in the fridge.*

Hands trembling, Hannah responds. *Mom, what's wrong?*

After ten minutes pass without a response, she grabs her backpack and goes to find Fiona.

* * *

They decide to leave school. Fiona suggests asking permission, but there is no one to ask. The teachers have vanished, and soon the hallways fill with confused and panicked students, all of them asking the same questions and getting no answers. Other kids opt to remain in their classrooms. They stare blankly at the chalkboard, or down at their hands. The door to the principal's office is locked, but through the frosted glass the girls see the warped figure of someone inside standing dead still, arms held aloft.

"This is fucked," Fiona says, a tremor in her voice.

"Maybe it was nerve gas or something."

"*If* it was anything at all and not just some kids playing a hell of a prank. Whatever the case, time to blow this joint."

They head for the main doors through a sea of students and panicked voices.

"The Internet's down," says one.

"Mine isn't," says another, "But there's interference. Lines across the screen. I can't make out the words."

"I saw the explosion," says a third. "Just for a minute before it cut out. The flames were green."

"And beautiful," adds the pale boy standing next to her. His smile is a terrible thing to behold.

"I gotta get home." Hannah's panic is reflected in the faces around her. Prank or not, and somehow that seems highly unlikely, something is definitely wrong. She can feel it in the air, can almost smell it. The air feels charged, as if a storm is coming.

"Okay. We can check on your Mom first. See if she's okay."

"And if she's not?" There are tears in Hannah's eyes at the thought of how dismissive she was earlier that morning. She hopes and prays her mother is all right.

"Don't think that way." Fiona shoulders aside a trio of girls who have drawn closer together to pose for a selfie. None of them are smiling.

*Hashtag, apocalypse*, Hannah thinks.

As they passed the gym, both girls see through the small wired-glass window all the boys lined up and facing the wall, their arms by their sides like soldiers at inspection. The gym teacher Mr. Burleson is nowhere in sight.

\* \* \*

On the drive home, there are few people on the streets. The sidewalks should have been alive with costumed ghouls, but the only evidence that it's Halloween at all are the decorations outside the houses and stores. Somehow their presence without people there to humanize them makes the streets look eerier still. It's as if a curfew is in effect, and Hannah can't help wondering if even now they are breathing in something deadly. Has there been an attack, an invasion, an outbreak? Why aren't the tornado sirens going off? Where are the police, the army, the emergency services they saw earlier?

As they pass the neighborhood where they were forced to park on the way to school, Hannah sees the scarecrow the mother and her children were so industriously stuffing has been rent asunder, the hay scattered all across the lawn and out onto the street. The old man's polystyrene zombie is still standing, and the old man himself is standing before it, mimicking it, his back to the street, arms down by his sides, unmoving.

"Where *is* everybody?" Fiona asks, which strikes Hannah as a very end-of-the-world kind of question to ask. Rather than attempt to answer, she gets out her phone. In trying to brush a loose hair off the screen, she realizes it is somehow under the glass and likely not a hair at all but a sign of something wrong with her screen. Her head starts to hurt. She has over a hundred text messages, none of which she was alerted to, and now the Wi-Fi symbol has a line through it. Next to it are the words: NO SERVICE. How then did the messages come through? She considers trying to search through them to see if there might be one from her mother, hopefully saying her phone was stolen or she had a brief stroke, or was in on the elaborate prank all of this must surely be, but she knows she'll be home in the time it takes her to scroll through them.

"Hey," Fiona says quietly as she steers the Camaro around a car that's stopped in the middle of the street. Inside, a man and a woman dressed in business clothes are staring out through the windshield and grinning vacantly up at the autumnal sun, their hands raised before them as if in supplication.

"Yeah?"

"I'm scared."

"Me too."

They hold hands in silence for the rest of the short ride to Hannah's house.

* * *

There is no one home, but someone, presumably her mother, has been there at some point, because the fridge door is wide open, and the contents have been dumped all over the floor. *We're going coming bringing us home come home there's lice in the fridge.*

"Well," Fiona says, "This probably isn't good."

Hannah searches the house and finds no evidence of life. As she paces around the kitchen, hands in her hair, dread in her chest, her phone begins to pulse in her pocket. She quickly withdraws it and checks the display, which flickers erratically as if the power is being drained. The word DAD flashes on the screen. For once, in the eight months since he walked out the door with two suitcases and a promise that it was only short-term, she is glad to hear from him.

"Dad?"

"Honey?"

"Oh God, Dad. Are you okay? Do you know what's happening?"

Her father's voice sounds as if it's coming from very far away. The connection hisses and crackles. "They will come for you, baby. They want to disconnect you so that you can see."

"What? I don't understand? Please just tell me what's going on!" She is crying now, big ugly sobs as the fear hits her.

"Andromeda is all hands but you can't see it unless you let them use their fingers to take your eyes. There's almost nothing of me left, but you should run and hide. You're already full of light, of love. You don't need theirs. I'm sorry, baby. I love you and I'll see you in the stars, my stars, they will try to disconnect you keep your eyes on the phone they nee—"

"Dad? Dad, are you there?"

The call devolves into static. Hannah looks at the cell. No signal again, assuming there had been one to begin with.

"That was...that was my Dad."

Fiona moves to her side. Numb, Hannah lowers the phone and looks into the terrified face of her friend, who swallows and nods toward the kitchen window. "We should go. Now. There's a man outside. A repairman, I think."

"Shouldn't we let him in? Maybe he knows something."

Fiona slowly shakes her head.

"Why not?"

"I only caught a glimpse of him, and...at first I thought he was wearing shades, but then I noticed the blood, and I think...I don't think he has any eyes."

For a moment neither of them can move.

It is the single knock on the door that sends them hurrying out the back.

* * *

With a gasp, Hannah wakes and looks around in a panic. She is sitting on the floor, her back against an armchair. Across from her on the sofa, Fiona has her knees drawn up and draped in a comfy blanket, her eyes on the TV, which is showing nothing but static.

"Fi?"

Her friend looks at her as if in a daze, her eyes red and raw from crying.

And with that the panic returns, dispelling the hope that the day's events thus far have been imaginary, nothing more than a surreal dream. Hannah sits up straighter. "What happened?" She remembers coming to Fiona's house, remembers feeling weak and sitting down on the floor while her friend went to look for her parents, but then she must have fallen asleep, a notion almost incomprehensible to her.

"Fiona, are they...?" She doesn't know how to finish the sentence. Before today she was just your average insecure, sulky but smart teenager waiting on the day when her body would quit betraying her, so she could live a life of social acceptance instead of feeling confined to a box. Now she has awoken into a reality in which questioning the well-being of her best friend's family is not only an imperative, but unlikely to yield a positive response. It's a reality for which she is ill-equipped.

"I don't know where Mom and Dad are," Fiona tells her, her voice hoarse. "But someone nailed all the gloves we own to their bedroom ceiling."

Slowly, Hannah crawls on her hands and knees to sit by her friend. She takes her hand and finds it cold. "And Max?"

At the mention of his name, Fiona starts crying and trembling uncontrollably. Hannah joins her on the couch and holds her until the worst of it subsides. When Fiona speaks again, Hannah is not sure she hears her correctly, and isn't sure she wants to.

"Max is in his room. I thought he was sleeping. Then I saw his hands. They were on his pillow. And Max..." She takes a breath deep enough to power the words. "Max was on the opposite side of the room."

It is an impossible idea to process, just the latest of many. Hannah feels as if the world is ending, that somehow some unknowable horror has been unleashed upon them. As a fan of post-apocalyptic movies and TV shows, she has often found herself wondering what she would do in such a situation. Ultimately the only cohesive verdict she has ever reached has been to ally and most likely seduce Norman Reedus from *The Walking Dead*. Because that would make everything okay (or at least make her the envy of those for whom her existence means so little.) But now that the end is here, with her family gone and people going crazy, what she feels is not bravado or fantastical lust, but unadulterated terror. So, she does what she has always done in trying times.

She takes out her phone.

The onscreen buttons do not respond to her touch. They don't need to. The screen is a shifting kaleidoscope of colors and messages, some of which make sense, most of which do not. It is a repetitive jumble of plaintive commands and fervent exultations. The end has come, but to some, it is only the beginning.

"I want to die," Fiona whispers.

"Don't say that. We're going to make it." Her words are automatic and empty.

Fiona snorts laughter in response.

Beyond the shuttered blinds, it is getting dark.

When the power finally goes out, Hannah is relieved to have her phone, which represents the only light she has left, the only light she is likely to see again. The silence makes the dark room seem like a womb.

At some point, Fiona rises wordlessly up from the couch and goes into the kitchen.

Hannah barely hears her friend's whispers, but then both the words and the quiet are shattered by the clamor as Fiona starts to dig through the cutlery drawer.

The phone blurs further through the tears in Hannah's eyes as she brings it close to her face.

*Andromeda is coming.*

*Our Gods, our fathers, have found us.*

Upstairs, the door to the attic falls open with a bang.

*Home, we are home.*

*My God, the COLORS.*

The retractable stairs release a tortured unoiled shriek.

*We are the Light. We are saved.*

*Their universe is in the patterns on our hands.*

Footsteps on the stairs. Silence from the kitchen.

*Keep your eyes on your phone. Don't let them disconnect you.*

And she does.

Until it too, dies.

# SOMEONE TO CARVE THE PUMPKINS

**I**S THAT HER?"

Joe nodded. "Told you, didn't I? A ghost. As real as you or me, just like I said."

Chuck frowned and hunkered down beside his younger brother. He felt ridiculous hiding behind the hedge like a kid running from bullies, but if the old lady really was a ghost then he didn't particularly want her dead eyes focusing on him.

"She doesn't look like a ghost to me."

Joe looked at him as if he'd just cussed their mother. "Are you crazy? 'Course she does."

"She just looks like a regular old lady to me. Besides, ghosts are meant to be scary. Why is she just sitting there instead of trying to scare people?"

Joe's watery blue eyes were wide as marbles as he nodded at the leafy wall. "She's haunting that house!"

Chuck raised himself up enough to peer over the hedge. His knees creaked in protest.

The full force of the cold October breeze made his eyes water. He blinked away stinging tears and looked across Maiden Street.

She was sitting on the porch of a house they had always thought long abandoned.

He found it a little strange that there were no pumpkins to detract from the oaken gloom of the old house. It was Halloween after all and even the weather was playing its part to establish a deliciously sinister mood; burnt-orange leaves skittered along the pavement like giggling children and misshapen orange heads with candles for brains dotted the decks and porches of every house along the street.

Every house except *hers.*

She sat on a rocking chair beside the torn screen door, knitting something that might have been a child's sweater but looked to Chuck like oatmeal hanging from wickedly sharp needles. Her pallid face was scrunched up in an expression of concentration or worry. Her clothes looked dirty and old, a black shawl draped over her bony shoulders. The longer he watched her, the more he convinced himself that Joe was wrong about her. She wasn't a ghost. If anything, she looked more like a witch.

"Where are the pumpkins?" he muttered.

Joe thumped a fist on the grass. "She doesn't *have* any pumpkins 'cause she doesn't *need* them. What would a ghost need a pumpkin for?"

"Maybe she doesn't believe in Halloween. People who don't believe in things don't usually celebrate them, do they?"

Joe, still crouched on the ground with his chubby fingers splayed between his legs like a catcher at a baseball game, chewed his lower lip.

"But she has to be a ghost, Chuck. I mean she sits on that porch day in, day out. Sometimes late at night you can hear them needles from all the way across town, click-clicking like nobody's business."

"You think she's a ghost because she likes to knit?"

The excitement on Joe's face faded a little and Chuck decided it couldn't do any harm to let his brother have his ghost.

"Okay, so she's a ghost and she's haunting our neighborhood and we're the only ones who know about it, right?"

"Right," Joe said with utter seriousness.

"Then we have to do something about it."

Uncertainty flickered in the vibrant blue of his brother's eyes. "What are you talking about? What can we do? We're just kids."

Chuck grinned inwardly. "I'm gonna go over and tell her she has no business knitting and scaring people if she's supposed to be dead."

Joe grabbed his brother's ankle. "No! She'll--" He shrugged and gesticulated with his grubby hands but the words wouldn't come.

"She'll what? If she really is a ghost then she can't do anything to me, right? All she can do is say 'Boo!'"

Joe tugged harder at his brother's jeans and Chuck pulled away from him.

"C'mon Joe! Why don't you come with me and we'll both tell her to go back to wherever her body is?"

Joe shook his head so hard and fast Chuck thought it would fly off. "I'm scared of her, Chuck. You should be too. It's not right to mess with ghosts."

Chuck felt a pang of pity for his brother and considered forgetting the whole thing, but his own curiosity compelled him to introduce himself to the old lady, if for no other reason than to ask why she didn't have any pumpkins out on Halloween.

"I'm just going to go say, 'hello'."

"Don't," Joe whispered.

"Aw c'mon. Don't you think ghosts have better things to do on Halloween besides sitting on old porches knitting?"

The sky over their heads was a cold gray, the wind moaning high above them as if caught in a snare of clouds.

Chuck sighed and tousled his brother's dusty blond hair. "Okay. If you stay here and be my lookout, I reckon I'll have nothing to worry about. You can holler if it looks like she's about to change into a monster or something."

Joe blanched. "Don't let her get you."

"I won't. You got my back?"

"Sure."

Chuck winked, straightened and stomped purposefully off toward the gap in the hedge a few feet away from his brother. He heard Joe muttering a silent prayer at his back and suppressed a grin. At the gap he paused and looked back. He could see Joe's eyes peeking over the hedge, one eyebrow raised as if asking if he had changed his mind. Chuck sucked air through his nose and stuck out his chest in a dramatic gesture for Joe's benefit.

Chuck looked across the road.

The old lady in the faded floral dress rocked slowly to and fro. The faint sound of clicking reached his ears.

He began to walk.

He knew he should be looking up and down the road to be sure there were no cars coming like they'd been taught but his eyes were fixed on the lady and the crumbling house.

The porch looked as if it could collapse at any given moment, finally succumbing to the voracious appetite of the weeds and switch-grass that grabbed at its latticed framework. Next to the rocking chair an empty yellow egg carton flapped mutely in the breeze and Chuck guessed some kids had probably dumped it there after bombarding the house with its contents. The brownish scabs he saw on the mildewed siding confirmed his theory.

Rusted paint tins clustered in the corner of the porch and the steps leading up to where the old lady sat gently rocking were splintered and broken.

*Not a ghost but not much of a housekeeper either.*

Chuck had reached the center of the road and suddenly the old lady stopped and looked up at him.

And he knew he had made a mistake.

*Joe was right.* He was a silly kid with a head full of silly notions but for once he was *right.* He knew it in that moment without a shadow of a doubt.

It was as if he was standing before the open door of a freezer, his body wracked with a sudden inexplicable trembling. *Oh no.*

There was a sound like long nails dragging down a chalkboard and the world dimmed as if an enormous shadow had swept across the sky above his head.

He tried to move. Couldn't. And *she* was staring at him.

He was vaguely aware of the old lady getting to her feet. She made a curiously human gesture of gently laying her knitting down on the seat behind her. But she was far from human.

Joe's voice: *Don't let her get you.*

Chuck tried desperately to close his eyes before terror blurred his vision.

He felt an odd tingling sensation as thin white rivers of electricity arced from his fingertips and vanished into the ground at his feet. Tingling, no pain. Joe was yelling but from oh so far away now.

The old woman stared at him with a parody of sadness drawn on her wizened face.

*I'm frozen in the middle of the road. I'm frozen because she put a spell on me and a car'll come along and kill me and--*

The paralysis broke, sound rushing back into his ears, lancing his brain and he cried out, fell to his knees on the white line in the center of the road.

The line began to glow.

And still the old lady did not move.

"Chuck!" Joe screeched in a voice choked with panic and Chuck turned to look at his brother. Joe was miles away; nothing more than a speck seen through a revolving tunnel of thorns, but one thing was clear as day: the witch was making him glow too. He appeared almost angelic, glowing from within like so many of those images he'd seen in the Good Book.

White sparks flickered around Joe's head like lightning bugs.

Chuck looked back at the old lady. Her eyes were a milky white and he was struck by what he read in them. Unbearable agony.

Her voice came to him like the dry rustle of dead leaves. "Chuck, come home."

He could sense the urgency in her, ethereal hands attempting to lock their fingers around his own. She wanted him.

*Company for the dead.*

"Nnnooo," he grunted through teeth that refused to open.

She wanted a boy, a soul, anyone.

*Someone to carve the pumpkins.*

He screamed and spun, the white line flashing, blinding, searing as Chuck and his soul ran toward the gap in the fence, to Joe who was screaming, screaming, eyes wide as his brother dove through the fence.

The gap swallowed them.

* * *

*I have no memory of what it felt like to live by time. To have my days and nights governed by something beyond my control.*

*I stand on this old porch and watch, listening to the dying screams of terror the breeze will soon carry away. And I wait.*

*They will come again, I know. They always come back, just never all the way.*

*I hate that I am a stranger to them. It shreds my heart that death has erased the familiarity from their fragile little minds. Now, they fear me. What kind of a* symbol have I become to them? I'm sure I'm better not knowing.

I sit back in my rocking chair, my toes holding me still as the breeze runs its fingers through my hair, but no amount of sympathy can make it better. The breeze can only assist in drying my tears.

I go back to knitting and whisper a silent prayer to whoever listens that Chuck will be brave again someday and find the courage to reach the steps. Close enough to see the love in my eyes.

The love I have kept for Chuck and Joe.

My darling children. Taken from me by a stranger and buried out there in some unknown place beneath the October sky.

Come home...

Come home to mother.

# HAVEN

IT'S YOUR MOTHER. I'M AFRAID SHE'S PASSED AWAY."
Yes, yes. Old news. Never once has he stopped to think about how odd it is that he is so certain. The knowledge was just *there*, shortly before the phone rang, manifesting itself as an ability to breathe unrestricted, to straighten his shoulders and not meet the resistance of her eternal gaze, to dust off a genuine smile and use it without feeling it ephemeral.

Gone, and the days that follow are among the most wonderful he's ever had. Scarcely had he dared to imagine the release could be so full, so overwhelming, allowing him to tread with lightened step and floating heart. He encounters strangers and rather than showing them the top of his head in a cowl of cowardice and shame, he beams at them and bids them the sentiments in accordance with the age of the day. That these greetings are seldom reciprocated bothers him little, for his resolve is growing ever more formidable now that he has only one shadow trailing behind him.

Gone, and the nights exude peace, the mattress accepting his tired bones like clay in the hands of a potter. His dreams are golden, exorcized of the heavy cloying darkness that was the signature of life with Mother. There is no doubt that he loved her, but she molded him into a creature of indifference, isolating him in his own little box of shadow where there was never room for any kind of feeling.

He suspects what little grief he feels at her passing stems from his being accustomed to her constant presence rather than any true emotion on his part. This suspicion in turn ignites guilt, but guilt is something he has learned to master and, aided by his newfound happiness, it is soon beaten into submission.

The celebration of her death is a tawdry affair and Tom finds himself at the hub of a ring of people he doesn't know, or care to. The minister is a patrician man at least twenty years his senior, all practiced smiles and Bible passages as he leads them in a chorus of emotionless verse that rises like startled ravens above the gloomy fall graveyard. The air smells of cold earth and dying leaves.

Tom weathers the condolences, secretly wondering what it is about death that leads people to the assumption that they can immediately insinuate themselves into the lives of the grieving. If anything, he finds a note of condescension in those voices, powered by the look of *there but for the grace of God* in their eyes. It sickens him and reinforces his need to leave as soon as this stunted procession of sympathy is over.

When the last bleak face has moved away, he stuffs his hands into the pockets of his dark overcoat and rounds the church, the sympathizer's last words to him carried on ill-formed tendrils of autumn wind, falling just short of his desire to hear them.

Grumbling, he slips through the wrought-iron church gate, the spire of St. Andrew's like a chiding finger at his back, reminding him who might be watching his disregard for all things sacred. The image weighs on his shoulders like the memory of the woman he has left behind him in the ground. A woman he scarcely knows.

\* \* \*

*He has come home to the house on Marrow Lane.*

*As expected, his mother complains about the length of his hair, how much weight he has lost and asks him why he has bothered to come visit her after so long an absence. Her frequent wincing and moaning about her incessant headaches render his excuses meaningless.*

*"They steal my sleep and it's getting harder to keep anything down."*

*"You need to eat to keep your strength up," he replies, feeling achingly redundant and thinking: Who is this woman?*

*Her dramatics are almost certainly a cry for attention, a trait not unknown to her and worsened by age. He delivers the customary platitudes and takes his leave of her, ushered out on a cloud of protest only silenced by the thick oak door of the house.*

* * *

Now, standing before that very same door, running a trimmed fingernail over the cracks and ridges in the wood grain, he ponders the irony of her death.

*An aneurysm. If it's any consolation, I doubt she felt a thing. It would have been very sudden.*

*I see.*

*Had she been complaining about headaches or dizziness lately?*

*No. At least, not to me...*

Realizing he might have been able to save her had he taken her histrionics seriously brings to mind a far darker question: *Had you known, would you have done anything?*

Brushing the thought aside, he opens the door of the two-story memory vault he used to call home. As he steps into the hall his senses hone in on the smallest, the slightest

*(Tommy, is that you?)*

of sounds. He waits, the dust settling around him in the chorus of quiet, ears attuned to the soundtrack of the old house. Eventually he straightens, exhales heavily, and continues down the hall until he comes to the living room.

From the doorway, he sees the familiar sight of the old 10" television set in the corner opposite. A miniscule and fog-shrouded representation of himself is all that's showing on the vapid eye of the screen as he enters the room.

The beige carpet knots itself beneath his shoes and he resolves to have it torn up as soon as he moves in proper. He suspects that foul, vomit-colored layer of shag is older than himself and he has hated it for as long as he can remember.

The same goes for the sofa, a bloated brown semblance of intestines passing itself off as Naugahyde. The upholstery is ripped, yellow foam winking lewdly at him from elliptical eye-sockets. *Gone,* he thinks, relishing the thought of being rid of these harbingers of memory.

His double shadow bids him look up and he nods at the imitation gold chandelier, missing two of its four bulbs, then down to the once white wallpaper, curling from the mildewed plaster beneath...*Gone.*

The photographs, sepia-toned and black and white depictions of stern-faced young men cradling even sterner looking women in their burly arms, people he has never met but who he assumes are his relatives...*Gone.*

Gone, gone, gone. All of it. Anything not immediately pertaining to *his* life will be dumped and with an abandon impervious to the wheedling pleas of sentimentality. It is after all, *his* castle now.

Grinning, he makes his way down the hall to the kitchen.

This room seems smaller than he remembers it and he wonders if it has shrunk in on itself after years of absorbing the auras of subconscious misery from the inhabitants of this place.

The lemon-hued walls seem to sag as he wanders around the room. He sniffs at the leaky radiator with the small plastic bowl beneath the tap to catch the water and shakes his head at the grease-smeared range, the picture on the wall above it speckled with spots so that the faces of the two watercolor children look positively leprous. A foul smell drifts to his nose from the trash compactor beneath the sink. He decides to investigate that some other time.

Against the far wall stands a simple pine table with three chairs and it is here his gaze stalls as the bloated corpse of memory rises to the surface of his mind.

*You're a dreamer Tommy, you'll always be a dreamer and a man who spends too much time in his own head never gets a goddamn thing done.*

*Don't talk to him like that.*

*I don't remember anyone asking your opinion, Agnes. It's a sweet life for both of you, living in your daydreams while I'm out busting my ass to put food on the table.*

Tom stems the flow of recollection, feels it swell against his resistance. The surface of the table is pitted with scratch marks and tiny holes where knives have been used to make a point. Coffee rings on the left—his mother's side of the table—stare up at him like blinded eyes. On the right, paler circles where his father lost himself in the liquid utopia of liquor.

And in the middle where Tom used to sit there is nothing.

He can almost see himself now—a young boy, eyes permanently narrowed in anticipation of a blow that could come at any time, skin sallow, devoid of the youthful glow typical of a child his age, sitting in a chair that only emphasizes his diminutive frame, his parents flanking him like birds of prey, always watching and waiting as if they expect something profound to trickle from his small tight-lipped mouth. But Tommy remains silent as much as possible. It is safer.

Shrugging off the memory, Tom shuffles over to the range and the bulbous white kettle, the base blackened by time and negligence, the handle loose, screws rattling. He opens it and angles it toward the naked bulb behind him. To his surprise it appears moderately clean. Nevertheless, he rinses it until he is sure nothing untoward will end up in his cup, fills it and lights the gas ring beneath, the thought of piping hot coffee staving off the unpleasant chill reminiscence has brought in tow.

Suddenly the blue flame beneath the kettle sputters as the kitchen door drifts open. He turns as it groans wide, allowing him to see down the length of the hallway.

*Damn it.*

The front door is standing open. He figures he must have forgotten to close it when he came in so drawn was he by the familiar. He stomps down the hall, grabs the door handle and is pushing it closed when a faint shuffling gives him pause. He listens, glances at his wristwatch: almost eight. Not an odd time for people to be out wandering, surely?

Peering around the edge of the door and out onto the cracked pavement reveals nothing except the lazy onset of twilight; the air is heavy, stars twitch into life in the vermillion canvas that hangs above Marrow Lane. A neighborhood dog yips and growls, yips and whines like a violin with ill-tuned strings. Someone yells: "shut that damn dog the hell up," and is ignored.

Tom frowns and shivers at the autumn chill insinuating its way through the fabric of his coat. Just as he is about to shut the door, he catches sight of an old woman standing by the streetlight a few feet down from his house, her hair a wild halo of sodium fire. She is dressed in nothing more than a housecoat and slippers and appears to be staring right at him, sending an unwelcome spark of unease through him and he backs away from the door, starts to ease it closed.

The old lady moves.

He pauses, one eye peeking through the inch-wide space between door and jamb, watching though now he feels as if he has donned a coat of snakes, his skin crawling as the shadow-faced woman moves along the sidewalk with short, stiff steps, the orb of fuzzy darkness hiding eyes that may or may not be fixed on him. She shuffles closer still and he realizes this is the sound he heard earlier. *Shhhnick! Shhhnick! Shhhnick!*

He wants to close the door, an action that will leave his sudden inexplicable fear outside with the old woman, but he is powerless to do anything but watch.

She reaches the mailbox—a simple black tin semi-cylinder staked in Tom's garden but jutting out over the pavement—and stops, cocks her head and brings a gnarled hand toward it.

*Is she pilfering the mail or what?* He wonders, his unease no less potent as the idea of confronting her is rapidly abandoned.

He hears the soft scraping sound of the mailbox door being opened and watches in disbelief as the old lady stoops down and peers inside. After a moment in which he imagines he can feel the victory radiating in icy waves from her skeletal frame, her hand emerges clutching a small white rectangle. Clutching the letter to her chest, she swivels on her heels and shuffles back up the street, passing through the orange glow from the streetlight much quicker than she had on her way to steal the mail.

*I should have done something.* He watches the shadows swallow her. *That letter might have been important.*

The kettle shrieks and jars the thought from his head.

\* \* \*

Later that evening, he stands at the threshold to a time capsule, held in place by a feeling of unreality that almost makes him dizzy.

Over the last few years his visits to this house have been infrequent and he has never stayed, had in fact come armed with a plethora of excuses should such a thing be suggested. As a result, he has never come upstairs and seen his old room.

He is shocked to find it is exactly the same, from the crimson toy chest at the foot of the bed to the Mickey Mouse wallpaper. His old teddy bear Rufus, now missing an eye, sits atop a once white pillow, arms splayed in frozen greeting. The carpet whispers as he advances further into the sanctuary of his childhood, head pounding, eyes wide with the strain of trying to absorb the sudden rush of familiarity.

A small oak desk, rescued from the local dump and restored to nothing like its former glory by Tom's father in one of his rare charitable moods, stands solemnly before the small white-framed arched window overlooking the neighboring rooftops.

Through one of the four panes, a thin crack like mercury lightning streaks an eternal path in the glass from top to bottom. Beyond that, the darkness rolls over the silent neighborhood, dampening the sounds of life and nodding its ethereal assent to the night creatures and the hunters waiting for their time to shine.

Tom shakes his head, looks down at the pockmarked surface of the desk and remembers... *Just as his father jabs the kitchen table with his knife or fork or the stub of his carpenter's pencil, so Tommy waits until he is alone and punctuates his own confused anger with the corner of a ruler, or pen, or...*

"Did I hate him?" Tom asks the empty room. "Did I hate them both and not know it?"

He kneels before the desk as if it is the armrest in a confessional, his knees quickly growing sore on the threadbare carpet. He studies the indecipherable doodles and unfinished scribbles printed on the table. Only one is clear and etched with an angry hand into the wood:

# H A V E N

This one he understands, even if he can't quite remember carving it.

In here, in this room, he had been permitted to believe the misery wasn't endless, that someday his father would arrive home wearing a smile in place of his ever-present scowl and smelling of wood and sawdust instead of whiskey. In here, solitude had provided the perfect movie screen for the illusions his hope projected and as long as he stayed here, nothing could break the spell imagination wove around him. Here was peace, love and happiness. Out there, over the moat and a million miles away, were misery, hate and pain.

Tom lifts his head and looks out at an encroaching darkness unique to the season. He pictures the dying leaves caught in a maelstrom, spinning round in a mindless vortex like lost souls and he realizes nothing has changed.

As he gets to his feet, he sees himself again, youthful body hunched over the desk, hiding the bruises on his face, weeping as he mourns the death of another fantasy at the vicious hands of reality.

He decides then that he will not stay here tonight. Even though he has long since dismissed the idea that adolescent fantasies can soften the edges of life, he doesn't want to sleep in a place where that very belief died.

This room is haunted, but not by ghosts. He can sense his childhood self here, the child that has stayed in this room, poring over the marks on the table, still hating the Mickey Mouse wallpaper, still trying to figure out why his daddy beats him while his mother watches with tears in her eyes. He is still angry and probably still dreaming of a better life he will never get.

"But my life did get better," Tom tells the silent room, surprised by the lack of conviction in his voice. The taste of stale coffee clings to the back of his throat as he swallows and turns to leave.

*Stop lying to yourself. This was the only safe place.*

The voice in his head is devoid of malice but filled with determination. He ignores it for it is just another unwanted memory and one he has the luxury of dismissing.

With a rattling sigh he slowly makes his way back downstairs and wonders if it might be better to put the house up for sale, to let someone oblivious to the horrid memories make it their home, someone immune to the tapestries of pain fashioned from the dust itself and the sting of sharp tongues still lingering in the air.

He thought it would be different coming back here, that his mother had been the only remaining anchor to a past too dreadful to contemplate. A foolish assumption.

If anything, her presence had allowed him to think only of her part in the shadow play that had been his childhood. With her gone, the curtains were thrust open, every room a set upon which the dramas of a miserable youth waited for an audience.

But the fact remains that he has no place else to go.

He supposes a few weeks here won't hurt, just until he comes up with something better. Perhaps an extended vacation, to clear his head and relax for the first time in as long as he can remember.

He stops at the bottom of the stairs, sure he hasn't heard what his brain is telling him he has. A few moments of listening yield nothing to confirm there has been any noise and the tension begins to ebb from his muscles. Then it comes, softly, seeping under the door like floodwater: *Shhhnick! Shhhnick! Shhhnick!* He doesn't move; waits instead for what he is now certain will follow.

A brief scratching like nails on a garage door.

Or an old mailbox being opened.

*This is crazy.*

It takes a great deal of effort for him to swallow the knot of inexplicable fear that has lodged in his throat but he is suddenly tired of being afraid, can't remember the last time he hasn't been, and a surge of uncharacteristic resolve brings him to the door, makes him wrench it open, propels him down the garden path and delivers him to the mailbox and the old lady standing before it.

She is peering once again into the bulbous darkness inside.

"Excuse me," he says, his voice brittle in the cool air.

She ignores him, apparently too intent on her felonious task, but this close he can see that she is a lot older than he first thought, the myriad lines in her sallow face retaining the shadows as if they are an intrinsic part of her. The black pools of her eyes are curved at the behest of a toothless smile as she retrieves her second prize of the night from his mailbox.

It occurs to him that he has seen her somewhere before but is not altogether surprised. Marrow Lane is a small neighborhood.

"Excuse me but what do you think you're doing?" He wants to tap her on the shoulder, to grab her elbow or anything that might bring her focus round to him, but for some reason he senses that touching her would be a dreadful mistake.

She is holding the small white envelope up to the streetlight and he has almost conceded, is in fact formulating a parting caveat when she suddenly turns and says: "You always had a great imagination, Tommy" before once again shuffling off into the shadows, leaving him helpless to do anything but watch.

"Wait, who are you?" he cries after her and she looks back over her shoulder at him, her face a creamy blur in the darkness but then even the shuffling ceases and the sounds of night rush back in.

Only the soughing of the wind answers him.

Frowning, he goes back inside.

*How did she know my name?*

\* \* \*

In the hallway, Rufus sits against the wall.

Tom stands paralyzed, the door clicking shut behind him, muting the wind.

"Hello?" he asks the hallway and thinks that if the teddy bear turns his head in response he will most certainly drop dead of a heart attack. While the old lady was bizarre, she certainly wasn't beyond rational explanation. This however, is dancing on the boundaries of sanity.

He clearly remembers seeing the toy seated on the bed in his old room. He hadn't moved it, would recall if he had. How then, has it ended up down here?

Horrible images of the teddy bear carefully navigating the stairs while he was outside flash behind his eyes and he scoffs, a little too casually and feels his hackles rise.

"To hell with it." He rushes forward and scoops up the stuffed toy, then marches up the stairs, the loud clumping of his boots deliberate and reassuring. If someone else is here, they will know he is coming and that he isn't happy.

He reaches the landing and takes a deep breath, steels himself for whatever he might find in his old bedroom. With his heart chiseling its way through his ribcage, he stalks into the room. And comes to a dead halt.

A little boy, sallow-faced and sheet-white, has replaced Rufus on the bed; an ugly bruise purpling his left eye and most of his cheek. He is dressed in Mickey Mouse pajamas, *Tom's* old pajamas and as Tom watches, the boy raises his hands to receive the bear. Despite the surrealistic feel reality has draped over its shoulders, Tom tosses the bear to the child and tells himself to remain calm.

"Who are you?"

The boy looks at the bear as if he's addressing not Tom, but the toy. "You know who I am. Who do I remind you of?"

In truth, this is a question Tom has been hoping the boy doesn't ask, because the answer is something he is not prepared to face so he says: "I don't know."

The child looks amused and Tom feels his nerves fraying at the edges, unraveling. "How did you get in here?" he asks.

"I'm the one who makes stuff up, not you. So, stop pretending you don't already know these things you're asking me."

To accept what is presenting itself as the truth, as reality, as normality is to Tom, opening the door wide to insanity. So, for now, he will keep on pretending that the child sitting on the bed is not a younger version of himself. He carefully makes his way over to the desk and sits down, his finger absently tracing the striations in the surface of the table that form the word: HAVEN.

"I couldn't do it you know," the boy says, fingering Rufus's eye. "I couldn't bring her back."

"Who?"

"Mom. I guess I thought I'd be able to. After all, I was able to make Gramma come back."

Tom feels his skin grow cold and the old lady at the mailbox flashes before his eyes. She had seemed familiar. Now he knows why, and it brings to mind the sepia-toned pictures of smiling strangers down in the living room.

Without thinking, he blurts: "But she isn't dead. She's in a home in Harperville."

The boy nods. "She found her own safe place. I brought her back here where she belongs though, just like I thought I could bring Mommy home.

Just like I brought *you* home."

Tom rubs a hand over his face and leans forward. "And who do you think *I* am?"

"Still pretending you don't know? You're me, the part of me that went on and left me behind, the part of me forced to leave the safe place. You're what escaped."

Tom chuckles at that but it is a sound so far from mirth it frightens him, and his face draws tight with worry. "This is madness, you do see that don't you? This is like a literal translation of what shrinks mean when they talk about people talking to them*selves*. I'm expecting to wake any moment in an asylum."

The boy looks at him, his coral blue eyes glistening. "You've often thought there was something missing in your life, haven't you?"

Tom says nothing.

"So have I." For the moment, the stuffed toy is forgotten. "I thought in here nothing could touch me and for a while it worked. I got to stay where it was safe while you carried on living in the real world, forgetting the make-believe and acting like everyone else. I tried to bring Mommy back when she died but it didn't work. Gramma came back, and you came back, even though you still won't believe."

"What do you want from me?" Tom asks in a voice little more than a whisper.

The child looks back to the toy. "My safe place is crumbling. I can't be here on my own anymore."

"Why? If you've been here this long..." *What the hell am I saying? Am I actually buying this?*

But what the child says next dismisses all doubts because in the instant the words reach him, he is once more afraid, a fear that transcends all others.

"Daddy came back."

It is irrational, but by now Tom is coming to expect nothing less. He gets to his feet and looks down at the boy, at the fear etched on his face, a terror so suddenly familiar and personal that he believes everything without question, simple as that. Denying this reality any longer will drive him mad.

"He hurt you?"

The child nods. "He slipped through once, when I fell asleep and forgot to close the door all the way. I woke up and saw him standing over me, just a large shadow with gleaming white teeth. Now, I keep the door closed." He looks toward the door and Tom follows his gaze.

"Will you stay with me?"

"I don't know." His eyes are fixed on the door. It's open just a crack, but that crack is now as deadly as a yawning abyss.

"There is nothing out there for you. You know that. You've felt it ever since you left."

Tom mutters agreement but can't look away from the door or the shadows crawling up the walls of the stairs beyond.

"Please."

He thinks of the word scratched into the desk, the word he carved there all those years ago when he believed it to be true. Now he realizes it still can be.

Three paces and he is across the room and slamming the door closed.

The boy looks at him and smiles. "We might not be able to keep him out forever."

Tom walks to the bed and sits just below the boy's slippered feet. "We'll see."

His eyes are on the door.

"I missed you," says the boy.

Tom tries to ignore the creaking of the stairs.

# HOW THE NIGHT RECEIVES THEM

*It is not how you walk, or where, or how far. It is all in the sound of the steps and how the night receives them.*

**C**ARRIE SHAKES HER HEAD and her hood chafes her cheek. She hates the coat almost as much as she hates the woman who forced her to wear it, but secretly she is glad of its warmth, no matter how heavy and uncomfortable it feels around her thin frame. A sigh sends a cloud rolling out to join the fog. The skin across her face feels tight, like new leather; her eyes water. Her lips are cracked dry and raw.

*It is not how you walk...*

The dense fog turns the night to silver as it smothers the moon and steals its light. The vaporous clouds are like damp kisses against her face.

The words the man said made no sense to her, and she wishes she could stop thinking about them. But every time she tries to focus on something else—like her mother's worsening habit—those words come again, speaking over unrelated images like a displaced narrator.

*It's a quote*, the detective, who she has come to call The Poet, told her when she'd queried their origin, *from the one and only poem I ever wrote.*

*It's beautiful*, she'd replied, though she wasn't sure that was true. She'd wanted to ask what the words meant but refrained from doing so for fear the man with the sad green eyes and hangdog face would consider it rude. All she knew for certain was that the words, whatever the meaning behind them, clearly had greater significance to him than they would ever have for her. *You should write more of them. Seems like you know how.*

He'd smiled then, his car moving alongside her, the window down, the lights picking up the first gathering wisps of fog. *Sometimes there's enough darkness in the world without adding to it under the guise of something pretty,* he'd said, and she hadn't understood that either. So, she'd shrugged, dug her hands into the pockets of her heavy red coat, and stared down at her feet.

*I think if you have that kind of a talent, it'd be a shame not to use it,* she told him.

The Poet had nodded, eyes distant. *All my talent, if that's what you'd call it, goes only one way these days. Into the worst kind of darkness. And no one ever tries to make something pretty out of it, because there's nothing pretty to be had. Just...darkness.*

*But you help people, don't you? Your job is to be a voice for those who can't speak for themselves.*

He'd smiled at her again, the warmest smile she'd ever seen from him, and nodded. *That's very profound. And true, I guess, though it doesn't always feel like it. Some of the time it feels as if we're just here to bear witness to the acts of monsters. To validate their efforts by seeing what they've done.*

He'd fallen silent, as he often did. She had less than a mile to walk, less than a mile in his company, but the silence as he accompanied her was so much better than the quiet when she was alone. The rustling of nocturnal animals in the brush between the trees, the grating shriek of possums, the sharp bark of raccoons, the clamor of deer as they fled at the scent of her, the imagined sound of footsteps lost in the echo of her own...none of these things seemed threatening when he was by her side.

Tonight, however, as she reflects on all he said the night before, she is alone.

The fog is thicker.

The silence, deeper.

*It is all in the sound of the steps...*

The cold tries to infiltrate her coat, tries to creep up her sleeves and down the open throat. She folds her arms and hugs herself tight. Drops from an earlier rain plop to unseen puddles on the road. Leaves fall wetly to the asphalt.

Half a mile to go...

Though there are no landmarks visible by which she might gauge her progress, she knows where she is. Every night for the past six months she has walked this road and the feel of it beneath her feet has become familiar.

A slight rise here as she passes the turnoff to the Lincoln Travel Center.

A rough, fissured patch there where half-hearted attempts have been made to repair holes in the road.

The sign telling her where she is: *Route 50*.

The hill, lost in clouds of gray-white, the graveyard somewhere beyond the phalanx of warped ancient trees to the right, hidden from view so travelers have no reminder that death sees this road and visits often.

She shudders at the thought of those silent plots, those vaguely human-sized mounds in the lush grass, those endless rows of chiseled names, all lost in the fog, but most definitely there, for they have nowhere else to be, and no place else will have them.

Behind her, lights blossom in the gloom. She looks over her shoulder but maintains her pace. She could not have slowed even if she'd wanted to. The distant sound of tires sizzling through puddles. The drone of an engine. She almost smiles, feels a small flutter of excitement in her belly as the car approaches, the lights bullying through the fog to find her. A faint squeak of brakes and the sense of weight pushing along beside her, the whirr of a window being rolled down. Then a voice. Her smile fades, the flutter dies. It is not The Poet, the detective, her friend. It is no one she knows.

"Hey there." A man's voice. Cheery, laced with concern. "Hey Miss, is everything all right?"

She ignores the voice, and knows she's being rude, but can't help herself.

She doesn't want to acknowledge the man because then he will talk and ask questions for which she has no answers. He will assume the role of guardian, and it does not belong to him. So, she walks, and bows her head, her hood hiding her face.

"Miss? Were you in an accident?"

She shakes her head. Maybe if he thinks she's okay, he'll leave her alone.

"Do you need a ride?"

Again, she shakes her head, and strains her ears, hoping to hear another car on the road. But there's nothing. The thought that he might not come tonight saddens her, so she quickly dismisses it. He will come. He always does. He'll come to see her home.

But she is running out of road, and the man she doesn't know is still watching her, his car keeping pace with her, his concern tangible, and vaguely irritating.

"Miss?"

At last she looks his way. The darkness inside her hood shields her for the briefest of moments.

"I can give you a ride if you like."

Then the moon penetrates the protective veil of dark inside her hood and the man's breath sounds like air escaping a punctured tire. He doesn't say anything more. Doesn't even pause to roll his window up. He just jerks back in his seat, hits the gas and the car roars away, spraying water and skidding on leaves, and then there is nothing but red eyes blazing in the dark. Suffused and muted, and gone.

The night grows colder, the fog so thick now that there is nothing to see but white. But she knows the road, knows the feel of it so well.

Sometime later, another car, and now she is nearing home. The road turns sharply to the left and she has almost rounded the bend when she hears an engine growling. A song, faint, turned low, and a window slides down with a hum.

Then he is there, and she allows herself a small smile.

"I was wondering when you'd come," she says softly.

For a moment, The Poet says nothing.

She risks a glance around the edges of her hood.

He looks almost ghoulish, bathed by the green glow of the dashboard lights. His face is sunken, his eyes dirty coins above bags heavy with regret. His thinning hair is unkempt, uncombed. The hand on the steering wheel is like a denuded tree branch, the thin fingers tightening, making the rubber squeak. He does not look at her as he speaks:

"*'It is not how you walk, or where, or how far. It is all in the sound of the steps and how the night receives them.'*"

She frowns, looks away and concentrates on the road. "Did you write that for me?" she asks.

"I didn't mean to let you down," he says, ignoring the question. "I promised I'd keep you safe."

"I know," she says.

"I couldn't."

"Did you write the poem for me?"

"We found them, Carrie. We found them all. He'd taken the...faces, but before he died he...told us where to find them."

"I don't want to talk about that."

"He made some kind of perverse mural."

"Please...don't."

He shakes his head. A sob escapes him. "'The Surgeon of Salem', they're calling him. He'll be remembered, you can be damn well sure of that, but you, and the others? Only we'll remember you, and that isn't right. He'll be remembered by his sins. The innocent don't even have their fa—"

Sobs wrack him; he struggles to compose himself.

Alarmed, she glances at him, then away as his eyes turn in her direction.

"When they bury you," he says quietly. "They'll bury you as you were in life, not as he left you in death. It's something, I guess."

"Tell me about the poem. Tell me what it means."

Another car swishes by, but it is traveling in the opposite direction, back where there is nothing but memory. Carrie sees the pale smudge of a woman's face studying them before carrying on.

"He wanted your beauty. Your identity. He wanted to take it from you. To own it." He dries his eyes on his sleeve, talks in a strained voice. "Why? For God's sake, why...?"

Ahead, hazy rectangular lights shimmer in the murk.

Almost home.

"I'll drive this road every night until I can't do it anymore."

She smiles. "I'd like that."

"I see you, you know," he says wistfully. "Just as you were on that last night, and I will always see you that way. You were the bravest, most stubborn girl I'd ever met. Maybe I should have tried harder to convince you not to walk alone."

She clucks her tongue. "But I'm not alone. I have you."

He stops the car and kills the radio. The night becomes a held breath, caught in the throat of fog.

With a shaky sigh, he leans forward, places both hands on the top of the steering wheel, then presses his chin against them.

The girl stops too. The amber lights ahead beckon.

She turns and steps close to the car, puts her pale fingers on the door and faces The Poet.

"Will you tell me what those words mean? What your poem means? Did you write it for me?"

"You're safe now," he replies. "No one will hurt you again." She stands there, smiling, watching the man who will never be frightened by the running darkness that fills her red hood, and she leans forward and kisses him softly on his cheek. He doesn't move, but his breath slows, and he turns, looks directly at her.

"I can't see you anymore" he whispers, the tears in his eyes trapping green light.

"It's okay. I'm almost home," she tells him, and thinks of her mother, whom she suspects will be drunk, and high, and not at all happy to see her.

"I think I might love you," she says as she gives the man a shy finger wave and moves away from his car, leaving him awash in the verdant glow until the fog erases him and everything else. Then she listens carefully to the sound of her footsteps, to how the night receives them, and hears nothing at all.

# TONIGHT THE MOON IS OURS

**E**VAN WAITED BENEATH THE COVERS FOR THE SOUND. When it came crawling down the hall, a dry rasping staccato snore unbecoming the eighty-year old woman who made it, he grinned and threw back the covers. The moon, high and round and pure, shone a spotlight through the large bedroom window, illuminating his scuffed sneakers and crumpled jacket on the floor beside him. He had gone to bed dressed to save time and unnecessary noise and in less than a minute he was ready, poised by the window, face raised to the moon.

From his grandmother's bedroom, the slumberous grinding continued. Tilting his watch to the light, he saw it was not quite eleven, and that was fine. Teeth clenched as if the expression alone might lessen the possibility of noise, he painstakingly lifted the latch, winced at the faint squeak, and eased the window open.

Night air, cool and crisp, assailed his senses, canceling out the musty air in the room. Grasping the edges of the wooden frame, he put a foot on the radiator beneath the window and pulled himself up until he was crouching on the sill. He held his breath, listening, half-in, half-out of the room. Something fluttered from the safety of the spruce trees at the bottom of the yard; the stream trickling down from the mountains chuckled its way through the ditch. His grandmother's overweight basset hound Lester grumbled in his sleep from inside the garden shed.

Evan turned his back on the moon and with hands braced on the sill, lowered himself to the ground. Again, he paused, sure as he was every other night that his grandmother was going to catch him sneaking out. After a moment, he slid the window back until it was almost closed, the gap left for him to poke the latch fully open when he returned.

With a hiss of triumph, he tiptoed to where the stream was toying with the light, crossed it via a small rickety wooden bridge his grandfather had made from deadwood, and was out into the fields, the grass glittering with frost before him.

* * *

His grandmother's house was separated from the rest of the village by a two-acre field owned by a local farmer, who used it for his horses. As Evan crunched through the cold stiff grass, the moon making it seem as if he was walking on diamonds, he imagined he saw the animals, proud and dark, lurking among the shadows woven by the bare chestnut trees at the far side of the field. But of course, it was too cold for them to be left out at night now. Still, when he strained his ears, he imagined he could hear them snuffling.

Ahead of him, the land dipped and became an oblong of darkness, the moon denied by the newly built community hall—a towering structure which exuded modernity and so stuck out as alien in a village as ancient as Touraneena. Evan didn't mind it so much; they held basketball and volleyball there on Saturday mornings and chess on Sunday evenings, and if his parents insisted on dumping him out here every weekend, every distraction from the dreary village would be a welcome one.

Next to the community center, a strip of fir trees divided a small playing field from the low-slung school. Upon reaching the firs, Evan halted and ducked down, peering through the branches past the schoolhouse to The Shelter, a long concrete enclosure with one open side segmented by pillars, where the children sat to eat lunch or play when it rained. He warmed at the sight of it. It was here, on his fifteenth birthday, among the litter, spent cigarette butts and used condoms he'd first taken a sip of alcohol (which had been terrible, but for the sake of machismo, he'd feigned enjoyment). It was here he discussed things that would have reddened his grandmother's ears had she heard.

It was here he'd had his first kiss.

Voices. He turned his head, hands gripping the warped bole of the tree concealing him and listened. The scent of sap assailed him, and he breathed it in. On the slight breeze, he recognized the lilt of Yvonne's voice and Colm's frantic, urgent whispering. The latter's panicked susurrations resolved themselves into a warning: *There's someone over there. In the trees! Listen!*

His friends. Clearing his throat and affecting a deeper, more authoritative tone, he emerged from the trees, stiffened his gait and said: "You there. What are you doing out this late?"

There was silence for a moment, then nervous laughter. "*Evan!*" Colm sounded deflated by relief.

"You nearly gave me a heart attack," Yvonne said. "I thought it was my father."

Evan stopped short of the threshold. He could not see Colm and Yvonne's faces. The roof stopped the moonlight at their necks, encasing their heads in shadow. But he could see enough to know that Yvonne was wearing no jacket, just the sweater he liked with the picture of an eagle caught in mid-flight. It was less the picture however and more the swell of her flesh beneath it that had gained his approval.

"Where's Bobby?" he asked.

"No idea," Colm said. "He wasn't around all day today, and there's no one at his house."

"Huh," Evan said. "You'd have thought he would've said something. It's not like him to miss out."

"Maybe he got caught trying to sneak out," Colm offered.

Evan nodded. "Maybe."

Yvonne snorted. "It wouldn't surprise me if he's still sore about you and Colm ribbing him over the fairy stone."

The fairy stone. Evan couldn't resist a smile and Colm chuckled.

"Are you serious? He asked for it, with all that crap about magical rocks. Jesus, c'mon. People stopped believing in that stuff about a hundred years ago," Evan said.

"Not in this village they didn't," Yvonne said, and he didn't like how serious she sounded. If she believed in fairy stones, then he realized he might have jeopardized his chances of ever ending up with her by making fun of Bobby.

"It's ancient thinking," Colm said. "Superstition started up by a bunch of drunk farmers with nothing better to do."

Evan agreed, but decided not to vocalize it. Instead, he sighed and turned to look out across the fields he'd just crossed. He was reaching into his jacket pocket for a cigarette when Yvonne said quietly: "What about those children then?"

"What children?"

"Alice McCabe's twins. They've been missing for a week now."

Colm chuckled, but it was devoid of humor. "Those kids were odd anyway and their mother is odder still. If I lived with her and that trumpet voice of hers, I'd run away too."

"You think that's what happened?" Yvonne asked, sounding desperate to believe it.

"Sure I do."

Evan flicked his lighter and flinched when a shadow flitted across his feet. No one had moved, so he blamed the flame and the breeze and lit his cigarette.

"What do you think happened to them?" he asked Yvonne, suddenly wishing Colm were elsewhere so he could comfort her in the manner he'd rehearsed every night in his fantasies since they'd first kissed three weeks ago.

"I don't know. Give me a cigarette."

He offered her the pack, then the flame. She took both and when the lighter flared, he saw her eyes were pools of dark. Her shadow tried to tear away but was anchored to her shoulders; it stretched up the graffiti-riddled wall until she let the flame die.

"I hate autumn," Colm said then, refusing the cigarettes when Yvonne offered it to him. "So friggin' cold."

Evan didn't agree. He loved autumn; the way the leaves turned a panoply of colors before the trees let them go; the earthy aroma the breeze ferried across the fields; the crackle of frost, the clean taste in the air, the way the streets looked after the rain had come and gone. It was second only to summer in his season of choice. Whenever he and Yvonne were alone, he liked it even more. It seemed to swirl around them with its cape of dead leaves, hiding them from the rest of the world.

"Let's go up to the stone," Yvonne said then and he looked at her.

"The stone? Why?"

"Because Bobby was so anxious for us to see it." The moon made ghosts of her breath.

Colm groaned. "But we've seen it before."

"Not at night we haven't. Not in autumn."

Evan frowned. "What difference does it make *when* we've seen it. Doesn't it look the same all year round?"

"Dunno," she replied. "But I've never seen Bobby as excited as he was about it the other night."

"Bobby's a lunatic," Colm scoffed. "He'd be amused by a donkey."

"No, he wouldn't," Yvonne said, a little too protectively for Evan's taste.

"Yeah, but..." he started to say and gestured emptily. "It's just a rock."

"How do you know? You're a city boy. I'd hardly call you well-versed in the ways of rural Ireland."

That stung him, and he didn't reply. The moon was a bloated thing, cold-eyed and staring. He blew smoke at it and sagged against one of the stone columns.

"It's freezing in here," Colm grumbled. "My fingers are numb."

"So, blow on them," Yvonne said bitterly.

Evan couldn't understand what had soured her mood so abruptly. They'd been up to the rock last week and he had admitted that yes, it looked funny standing in the center of an otherwise empty field and yes, by all accounts gravity should have taken it down a long time ago so narrow was its base compared to the bulk that comprised the rest of it. Bobby's theory, culled straight from the cluster of bucolic locals in Brannigan's Bar, was that the rock was held in place by the power of the fairies that lived beneath it. Like a plug, he'd said, which had elicited a particularly crude sexual remark from Colm that had set all but Bobby laughing. They'd left shortly thereafter, Evan and Colm still giggling.

Afterward, Evan had recalled the conviction on Bobby's face and found it hard to believe anyone could subscribe to such preposterously outdated notions. He'd found the mental image of the four of them standing there yelping and batting at a swarm of tiny lute-carrying winged things utterly hysterical.

But Yvonne was in a stubborn mood tonight, and he had to inwardly throttle the voice that suggested she might have fallen for Bobby instead. After all, Evan was only here Fridays and Saturdays, which if nothing else granted him two days respite from his parents' endless quarreling. But it never occurred to him that Bobby might be in the running for Yvonne's affections, or worse, that she might consider him. He wasn't what Evan would term 'handsome' if forced to make a judgment, but Bobby did live in Touraneena, which gave him the advantage, if that was indeed what was afoot.

Evan decided the best thing to do before the damage became irreparable, was to acquiesce to her request, to do his best to seem on her side, which of course, he was. It was the superstition fueling her request that he questioned.

"All right let's do it," he said, dropping the cigarette and mashing it into ephemeral fireworks.

"Great. Outnumbered," Colm said with a sigh.

"You'll be okay," Yvonne said. She sounded pleased. "I'll look after you."

"Haw-haw."

Yvonne rose from the bench, rendering herself all but hidden by the dark.

"Come on then," she said. "Tonight the moon is ours."

Colm merely grumbled, but Evan wanted to ask what she meant by that. *Tonight the moon is ours.* It was a curious phrase, but he supposed she'd picked it up from one of those sickly-sweet romantic comedies she liked so much. In his pursuit of her, he'd even agreed to accompany her to one. *Waiting to Exhale*, it had been called though a more appropriate title might have been *Waiting for the Credits*. He had only managed to suffer through it by stealing sidelong glances at Yvonne, who was so engrossed in the movie, she hadn't noticed.

*Tonight the moon is ours.*

He liked that, but when he opened his mouth to tell her as much, he realized she hadn't waited to hear it. Neither had Colm.

He was alone, but for the cataract eye of the moon.

* * *

They were already in the field across from the school when Evan reached the stand of firs.

"Hey, wait for me!" he called, trying his best not to sound nervous, which he was. The speed with which they'd left him hinted at a plot; he sensed a prank ahead of him. Why else would they have scampered so fast? The paranoia theme park in his head was growing popular, so much so that he had to make a concentrated effort not to heed the whispers that told him there *was* no prank, that the only thing he had been left out of this evening was Yvonne's heart, which she might have given to Colm. But at the sight of them halting, he felt a welcome wave of reassurance. He hadn't known any of them that long, but conspirators they most certainly were not. And Yvonne loved him, no matter what vibes she might be transmitting tonight. She was forward to a fault, something that was not always the easiest thing to bear, but at least he could be sure that if her feelings had changed, he'd already know because she'd have told him.

*Unless she's waiting to get you alone before she breaks your heart.*

He shook his head and concentrated on the sound of the frost crunching beneath his shoes. The breeze strengthened and carried invisible slivers of ice to his skin. He shivered. When he looked up again, Yvonne and Colm were closer, and watching his approach.

Their faces looked like moons, bleached white and featureless but for snatches of shadow.

"Hurry up," Colm said.

"Yeah, c'mon snail-trail," Yvonne added, and they turned away, just as he was within whispering distance of them.

"Are we in a hurry?" he asked, and now the sound of them trampling the iced grass seemed almost loud enough to wake the village.

"No, but it's cold," Colm replied.

Evan jammed his hands in his pockets and found himself taking longer strides to keep up. Colm was right; it was cold, so cold he had to duck his chin into his coat for fear it would freeze and drop off. To his right, beyond the low fence, his grandmother's house could be seen – a silent shape with black eyes for windows. He felt a surge of relief, as he always did when he came home after a late-night rendezvous with his friends and found the house asleep. Darkness meant he'd gotten away with it again. A burning light meant someone had woken up. A light meant trouble.

Colm and Yvonne were still ahead of him. They were close enough that he could reach out and touch them, but he found he was unable to draw level with them without breaking into a jog.

"Scare you back there?" Colm said.

"No. I just thought you guys wanted to be off by yourselves that's all."

Colm breathed laughter. "That'll be the day."

Yvonne said nothing.

At last they stopped at the edge of the field where the horse chestnut trees shattered the moon and made broken spider legs of the shadows. Here the grass became a short stretch of frozen dirt that led to a moss-skinned stone wall topped by rusted loops of old wire, presumably to keep the horses from clearing the fence when the mood struck them. Without a word, and before Evan could suggest a few moments to catch their breath, Colm was scaling the wall, carefully ducking under the fence, then gone, his feet thudding down on the earth on the opposite side.

"You coming, folks?" he called back. The breeze filtered his voice through the stirring branches above.

Yvonne turned to look at Evan. The moonlight streaming through the trees made sapphires of her eyes and an unflattering gray patchwork of her skin. Her hand fell on his wrist.

"Are you okay?"

His gaze dropped to her hand. Her grip was tight. "Sure. You?"

She smiled, and the expression seemed to chase the peculiar cast from her face.

In the trees, a bird flapped its wings in irritation. On the other side of the fence, frosty earth gave way beneath impatient shoes.

Colm's disembodied voice floated over the wall. "What's going on?"

"Nothing," Yvonne said. "We're just having a tender moment."

Evan's heart kicked. He smiled. "Is that what this is?"

She stepped close and he stiffened.

"Maybe."

Colm's grumbling.

A snuffling of horses Evan knew was only in his head.

The gentle soughing of the wind.

The shadows, shifting. Stirring.

Branches tapping together like dry bones.

The kiss, soft and cool on his lips but fantastically hot inside him as wild flames poured through his chest and down into his groin, where another reaction began to take place.

And then she was stepping back, her amusement little more than a shadowy curve in the stark oval of her face.

"Easy, tiger," she said and giggled.

Evan blushed then shifted his stance when her back was turned. He watched her grab the crumbling fence, her slender wrists exposed, made ivory by a swatch of moonlight, her dark hair flowing around her...

...And knew he was in love. Knew he wanted to kiss those wrists, those hands... every part of her. Knew he would have to confront her, maybe tonight if the opportunity arose, and find out exactly how much she wanted him. If it was even close to how he felt for her, if she entertained even a fraction of the desire that raged within him, then he would be entering uncharted territory, and the idea of it thrilled him. The idea of lying with her, her milky body spread out before him, his alone, free to touch, to kiss, to taste, sent shivers coursing through him, shivers that settled in his belly and stayed there like moths in a jar.

Yvonne topped the fence, loose stones clacking to the ground in her wake. She looked over her shoulder at him, the moonlit sky over the field beyond making a simian silhouette of her lithe body.

"Hurry my love," she whispered, and dropped out of sight.

*Hurry my love.* A trick of the wind, he knew, but dared to hope otherwise; and though that hope was feeble, he tackled the wall like a maddened thing, barking his shins, scraping his elbows, feet scrabbling against stone, hooked hands tearing clumps of moss free, until finally he was on top of the wall and surveying the flat glistening emptiness on the other side.

In the distance, at the far side of the field, the peaked roof of an abandoned barn peered at him from between fingers of spruce. Above it, the moon beamed through scudding clouds like a headlight in the fog, bleaching out the stars.

And in the center of the glittering field, a rough triangular shape rose and shunned the light. From here it looked almost like an oversized coffin, with a head too wide and a bottom too narrow. He wondered again how the slightest breeze didn't send it toppling. He estimated the middle of it to be about ten feet across. From there it tapered to a point no more than a few inches wide. By all rights, it should be lying on its face, but according to all who knew it, it had been there for as long as anyone could remember.

"I wonder why the farmer never tried to get rid of it," Evan whispered, and waited for an answer. When none came, he squinted into the gloom at his feet and saw nothing.

"You there?"

A ruffle of feathers was the only response and it came from the network of branches over his head.

He was alone.

Fear thrummed through him, but he maintained his composure, not wanting Yvonne to see his true reaction to what was almost certainly a scheme to spook him. After a few minutes of listening to the rasp of his own breathing and watching the ghosts of his breath tearing themselves asunder before him, fear became irritation. He balled his fists to keep his hands from trembling. Was Yvonne just teasing him, then? Was that all this was: a joke? He desperately wanted to believe it wasn't, that she really loved him. Maybe Colm had talked her into giving Evan a good scare. If that's all it was, then fine, despite it seeming immature, even for Colm. He wanted to creep back in his window to bed tonight and lie there knowing that she loved him. He was more afraid of discovering the opposite was true than he was at finding himself suddenly and inexplicably alone.

Then he saw them. They must have been crouching in the darkness somewhere because there they were, not ten feet away, standing stock-still and watching. It puzzled him that he hadn't spotted them before now. Still, he didn't dwell on it. Maybe a cloud had passed over the moon and shaded them from view for a few moments. Whatever. They hadn't abandoned him and that's all he cared about. It was clear they weren't trying to scare him either. There was no jumping out at him, no mournful wailing, no waving arms or hands clamping on his shoulders. They just stood there, waiting. With a sigh so heavy with relief he was sure they'd hear it, he slid down from the wall and began to walk toward them.

The wind rose, sending frost-hardened leaves skittering across the ground. A trio of ravens took to the air at the far side of the field and cawed their way past the moon.

Something whickered in the shadows.

Evan reached Yvonne and Colm and half-heartedly chastised them for being too impatient.

Colm looked back at him, only the slope of his cheek catching the light.

"We weren't sure you were coming."

"And let you steal my woman?"

The silence was deadly.

Evan chuckled to show he was joking, but the sound died in his throat.

There were two vertical strips of frost, like snail-trails, on the back of Colm's jacket, as if he'd been lying belly up on the furrowed earth.

Lying on his back.

It was nothing, he decided. He was being ridiculous. Colm might have fallen or been loaned the crystals from a low hanging branch when he'd scaled the wall.

Or from when he'd been hiding.

With Yvonne.

Despite his resistance, the certainty that he was being deceived overcame him. A cold knot of hurt tightened his throat and he allowed himself to fall back a few steps. It wasn't hard. They were walking too fast for him anyway. Tears stung the back of his eyes. He felt hollowed out, the butterflies in his stomach raising hell with razorblade wings.

It was all too clear now what they were up to and he felt like an idiot for not having seen it before. They weren't trying to scare him, not on purpose anyway. They were trying to ditch him. So they could be alone. In the dark. Colm and Yvonne. Doing the very thing he'd hoped to find himself doing by night's end. The very thing he'd dreamed of doing.

*Tonight the moon is ours.*

Yes, but not *his*.

Suddenly he wanted to turn and run, back to the wall, back to his room and sleep and morning and the ride home that would await him by noon. It would suit him never to see this godforsaken village or anyone in it ever again.

The splintering of his heart might have been that much easier to bear if not for their sneakiness. Without warning, he'd been relegated to third wheel, Yvonne's flirtation with him now insulting rather than titillating. Then he thought back to The Shelter, when she'd suggested visiting the stone, and realized she might not have been looking at him when she'd said it. He remembered the ease with which they'd hurried away from him, leaving him standing there. And then again at the wall. He had mistakenly assumed he was part of the equation when, he'd insinuated himself into a seduction ritual that did not include him.

As he plodded along behind them, he saw ice catch the light in streaks across Yvonne's back too, and that sealed it. The image of them cavorting in the shadows, their bodies tight together while they listened for Evan's approach, for their cue to act like his friends once more, infuriated and sickened him at once.

He stopped and kicked at a nub of packed earth.

Yvonne and Colm stopped too and turned.

"What's the matter?" Colm asked, and wasn't there the slightest touch of smug satisfaction in his voice?

"You chickening out on me?" Yvonne said and though he couldn't see her smile, he could feel it. His face grew hot. He wanted to hurt them, to show them he wasn't the poor fool they obviously thought he was. Instead, he shook his head.

"I just don't see the point of this, that's all," he told them. The wind drew icy fingers across his scalp.

"Don't be such a wimp," she said and lunged forward, her pale fingers finding the folds of his coat and jerking him forward hard enough that he yelped in surprise.

Colm laughed.

When she released him, Evan stumbled back into mercilessly cold shadow. The fairy stone: an ugly featureless rock, unremarkable save for its new identity as the place where his pride had taken its fatal strike.

"Lighten up a little," Colm said, his voice still infected with mirth.

Evan raged, trembling so violently he had to reach a hand out to the stone to steady himself. The rough surface scraped his fingers.

Yvonne, bathed in moonlight, was smiling.

"Don't ever do that again," Evan said, mustering as much threat as the pain and betrayal would allow without reducing him to tears. The night had turned rotten in a heartbeat, his hopes shattered into dust and now Yvonne had delivered the final insult by tossing him around like a lackey. He wanted to go home. Home, where his real friends were. Friends who wore only one face.

"Everyone knows," she said then, and might have added something but it was lost in the beating of wings, somewhere in the trees.

A faint mist curled at Evan's feet, the breath of the moon.

Colm was still chuckling. Evan considered smashing his face in but decided that would achieve nothing but further trouble. And yet, he knew how satisfying it would feel to hear that bulbous nose giving way beneath his fist. Yvonne would scream and try to intervene and maybe, just maybe his fist would fly wide of its mark and...

*Everybody knows.*

Everyone but Evan had known how sly his two friends were. Even Bobby knew. They'd played him for a fool, getting their kicks from the city boy to alleviate the monotony of country life. He supposed Bobby's superstition had been an act also, designed to make him look silly. Well, in that, they'd succeeded.

Then he heard it again, the snuffling of horses but pushed it away. His heartbeat thundered in his ears, fists clenching and releasing. He was not welcome here and had never been. Fine. They'd had their laugh. It was time to end it.

"But no one can tell," Colm said, jovially. "That's the only rule, you see."

Back at the fence, shadows poured over the wall and lingered there.

The mist spun and curled.

Wings.

"Oh, don't worry," Evan said with a bitter grin. "I won't tell anyone what conniving fuckers you people are. That's your own business. I just hope it was worth it. Next time you're in Dungarvan, look me up and I'll show you how us city folk play the game."

Yvonne was still smiling that infuriating smile.

"Bobby knew," she said, "but he wasn't supposed to tell."

The clouds tore apart in the hands of the wind and clean white light fled across the field in pursuit of the dark. It lit the trees, frosting the branches. It lit the mist, and the horses standing there held still by their riders.

Evan blinked, rubbed his eyes and looked again. The field was suddenly crowded but only in the corner of his eye. When he gazed upon them fully, the horses, lathered and snuffling, and their riders, tall and staring, were lost in the haze.

Waiting.

"The McCabe twins were here too," Yvonne continued. "They knew, but despite our warnings, they told."

"What are you talking about?" Evan said, wanting to run and be away from these awful people at last. They'd tricked him, used him for their amusement and crushed his dreams in the process. What else could they do to compound his misery?

Hooves pawed the ground.

A fluttering, but no longer in the trees.

The moon, an opaque eye.

And two figures, standing before him, smiling. Smiling at the fool, even as the moonlight turned their skin to sagging parchment tattooed with hate, even as their smiles became hooked, frozen things, even as their eyes sank in their sockets and caught blue fire.

"Stop," Evan said, stumbling back until he collided with the stone. Its shadow swept cold arms around him, held him still, but couldn't stall the trembling.

Another joke, ha-ha.

But it wasn't, and he knew it.

They stepped closer. The mist rose, caressing their smooth, supple bodies, now exposed and whitened by the moon. They were sexless things, he saw as he wept. Sexless, and heartless. When Colm turned his suddenly hairless head to address the riders behind him, Evan was not entirely surprised to see translucent wings struggling outward from the lines of frost on his back. They trapped the moon and fractured it, projecting an array of colors unlike anything he'd ever seen, or wanted to see. They beat once at the air, a single flutter, and Colm vanished into the mist. When Evan saw him again, he was mounted on a steed that seemed composed of spider web and glass.

The gathering was quiet.

Evan sobbed, the cold creeping inside him.

Yvonne was standing before him, tendrils of mist drifting toward his face from her glittering lips. Her eyes were moons.

"Tonight," she said, "I'm yours."

# THE TOLL

**W**HEN MILES CAMDEN AWOKE TO FIND HIMSELF, not in his bed as he'd expected, but rather sequestered in a pine box, his first reaction was not panic, or terror, but amusement. In truth, he had wondered somewhat idly over the past few months when his enemies would finally gather up the courage to make their move against him, and when they did, just how they would go about it. He had, however, anticipated something less dramatic. Poison, perhaps, or a pillow over his slumbering face, or a well-placed hand between the shoulder blades that would send his wheelchair-bound form tumbling down the winding marble staircase of his estate.

So, to wake in a coffin, while certainly an unpleasant and inconvenient development, certainly came as no surprise, no more than living under heavy gray clouds for a year only to wake to find it raining. But it was also somewhat disappointing. Whoever his enemy might be, they had chosen to imprison him rather than kill him outright, and not only did this speak to their cowardice and slow-mindedness, it testified to their complete lack of understanding of Camden's character. For he had already been imprisoned for years in his own fortress, either in the plush vault of his chambers—the heart of the mansion's opulent body—or in his mobile chair, limited to tired exploration of familiar rooms. He had grown accustomed to his comfort being tenuous by virtue of its dependence on others, his movements facilitated by sour-looking servants, his survival reliant on the whims of strangers.

And while he applauded his captor for being kind enough to provide him with a source of illumination, to Camden, it was a further sign of weakness, a gap in the kind of armor essential for any man to appear without mercy. If Camden put himself in the captor's—no doubt cheap—shoes (for he had already assumed the motive to be monetary), he would have ensured his captive awake in disorienting darkness. Then again, he had to concede that the lantern, placed in the far-left corner of the box by his foot, provided complications of its own. For one, the paraffin produced threads of oily smoke that had already filled the coffin, making it difficult to draw a breath that didn't taste like a coal-miner's sleeve. In addition to polluting the air, it would also be using it to stay alight, and without knowing whether the coffin had been buried, Camden couldn't predict the volume of oxygen he had to share. If he had indeed been interred (which would suggest a smidge more nerve than his captor's yellow disposition had heretofore suggested), then Camden was glad that the lantern was enclosed at the top, for its flame might have burned through the lid of the coffin, and the old man was not confident that his ninety-pound frame could withstand the sudden introduction of hundreds of pounds of clay into the pine enclosure.

Then, as if to put to rest the question of burial, an involuntary rattling cough was answered by a groan from the lid above him and he heard, rather than saw or felt, a trickle of earth between his bare feet.

He gave a small shake of his head. *Brazen.* And something tickled his cheek. His confinement allowed little more than a shrug of recoil, and he quickly turned his head to the right, expecting to see a spider previously only glimpsed on the covers of pulp horror magazines, an arachnid black as night and the size of a man's fist, raised forelegs presaging attack and a slow, painful death.

What Camden saw was not a spider, or any such terrible beast, but a cord, a mere string still shuddering with the vibrations of his own fear, and he allowed himself a grin, both at his own foolishness—exacerbated by his circumstances and the fact that when last he had seen his house, it had been festooned with ghoulish decorations appropriate for the Halloween season—and at what he deemed yet another faux pas on the part of his captor.

If this century was to be known by anything other than its fair share of atrocities and diseases, then surely the gullibility of the weak-minded would qualify as a footnote. Inflamed by the cholera epidemic, and Camden supposed, aided in no small part by Poe and his miserable, hysterical and depressing tales of premature burial, the idea of "safety boxes" had crept into the frail, common consciousness like a burglar into a shoddily built house. Fear of disease had been subverted and exacerbated by a fear, not of death, but of the preposterous notion of a kind of *un*-death, which left you wide awake and clawing at your coffin lid long after your mourners had departed the graveyard. To pacify such fears, coffin-makers had begun to include their boxes with cords that led up through the earth to a little brass bell, so that one could, upon awakening to find oneself a product of erroneous interment, yank on the cord, and alert the graveyard watchmen to the problem. That his captor had included such an inane device and put him in the ground on Hallows Eve, told him that his enemy was equally trapped by superstition. That they had buried him in such a cheap coffin, ill-befitting a man of his reputation, spoke to their bitterness.

Camden chuckled. The lamplight fluttered, causing ghoulish shadows to spring at him in the impermanent gloom. More dirt trickled into the box from the unseen fissure somewhere near the bottom. Camden coughed and lowered his hands, turned them palms down by his sides in imitation of repose. He sighed and watched the caul of smoke whip itself away from him. His eyes were beginning to sting. He closed them, content to pass a few moments pondering his captivity and those responsible.

Envy and enmity were directly proportional to the amount of wealth he had accrued in his four decades as a textile magnate. Interest earned was another enemy gained. Some of these enemies he knew as competitors, political opponents, or even former friends with whom he had severed ties on the eve of the realization that the return on their friendship did not equal the investment. He was not given to charity, particularly for those whose need stemmed from an unwillingness, rather than any inherent inability, to help themselves. Such people better suited the classification of the mythical un-dead, forever ringing a bell in the hope of being saved, when above ground they had seldom tried to save themselves. These people repulsed him, and deserved their fate, whereas Camden believed his current predicament was merely yet another in a long line of unfair side-effects of his having worked obsessively to safeguard his own.

It was not easy to select the most likely culprit from the list of them. A lifetime of success, of ruthless double-dealings, buyouts and layoffs, had made him distinctly unpopular among those with whom he'd dealt. His peers, on the other hand, those similarly well-versed in the methodology of good, unsentimental business, considered him a threat to their own empires, though in truth he had never kept more than a half-eye on them, and this mainly so he could be sure they kept to their own domains.

He withdrew the lighthouse beam of his focus to closer shores. When he considered it, he realized there wasn't one among the staff at Camden House that he could credit with enough brass or ingenuity to propagate such a stunt. Even though he had a policy which required them to taste in his presence the food they served him, it was a medieval ritual intended more to remind them that they did not, and never would, have his trust, than out of any real fear of mutiny. They were loyal, he knew, and even if they did not care for him or enjoy working for him, the compensation they received for doing so was more than fair, and better than they would get elsewhere given their qualifications. And if they left, as a few had done before, Camden's name was well enough known that they would have to travel far to find a house that would employ his hand-me-downs without worrying that it would cause offense. Which of course, it would not, but such fears were what kept employees where they were, and spared Camden the chore of having to replace them.

With the staff dismissed from consideration—the irony being that if it should resolve that someone in his employ had indeed possessed the salt to engineer such a bold action against him, they would undoubtedly have earned his respect—and with all his kin deceased, he turned his mind to romantic associations. And here, the list was a short one. Of the three women he had married and subsequently rejected, primarily because love for success seldom left ample room for love of any other kind, at least in the eyes of his brides, a contention he had never debated due to insufficient evidence to the contrary, only one was still alive. He still felt affection for Rebecca, and only Rebecca, not least because their dissolution had been the least combative and ugly, but because, although he wasn't sure he was capable of love, at least not in the doe-eyed, illogical and deranged way dictated by those fool romantics, he felt he had come closest with her. Initially, he had courted her purely to undermine a business rival—her father, but quickly and unexpectedly, he had developed a fondness for her. Unlike his other wives, Veronica and Bronwyn, whose hearts had been won only by the dual suitors of financial security and societal prestige, Rebecca had invested her love in him, believing that somewhere behind the callous armor, Camden was a good and loving man. She contended that he had worn this suit for so long that it had grown rusty and familiar, had fused itself to his skin. She was confident that she could find a way to penetrate that armor. A decade of trying wore her down, but my God, how he had loved to watch her try. How he had enjoyed listening to her speak, and sing, and read aloud from Shakespeare and Wordsworth and Auden and Austen in a library that seemed only to exist because she had breathed something of herself into the room. How he had struggled to suppress a smile at the sight of her frustration when she vied for command of the kitchen with the dour old cook and the resulting meal was unsatisfactory.

In the end, showing every line and wrinkle of her ten years of trying to reach him, she had touched his face and told him that she was leaving. "You're a candle with the potential to outshine all others," she'd said. "But your wick is made of wire. No matter how close I bring the match, it refuses to accept the fire." When Camden asked her from which of her favorite poets she had taken this quote, she had simply smiled at him and brought his hand to her breast to hear the origin of the verse for himself. The she was gone, with a promise that she would not be looking to him for support of any kind, which she had kept, and promises to stay in touch, which she had not. And he missed her.

He opened his eyes and told himself that the single stray tear that trickled down his cheek was due to the smoke, which had grown thicker and more noxious.

Such cruelty, as his captor would undoubtedly consider their amateurish attempt at extortion, was so far beneath Rebecca that he chastised himself for even thinking it, however fleetingly. Of the other ill-advised unions, both the result of promises made on nights in which his mind had been clouded by brandy, opiates, and the attention of women whose sexual prowess would have humbled him into acquiescence no matter what their demands, he considered only one a viable candidate for such unpleasantness: Bronwyn. Veronica had simply lacked the intelligence necessary to engineer such a loathsome revenge.

At the thought of Bronwyn, he felt his shoulders tense, the wood beneath him chafing the skin of his clenched fists. Bronwyn Connors, or as he had learned to refer to her when forced to refer to her at all: "That Welsh-Irish Mongrel Whore". He had met her in a tavern in London, England while on vacation with his first wife Veronica. While his wife had been laid up in their hotel room, sickened by what she referred to as a "putrid sewer-stench fog", he had let himself be seduced by Bronwyn, even though it was never far from his mind that likely she would expect payment for any time they spent together. As it turned out, she was not a prostitute at all, at least not in any official sense, and after their passionate and somewhat perverse night in her cheap, rented room, he had drunkenly confessed to her not only his dissatisfaction with his current wife, who with each passing day seemed to be abandoning the traits that had initially drawn him to her (traits closer to Bronwyn's at the time, if he was honest) in favor of affectations that neither suited nor complimented her, but also his address. And she had followed him back to Nottingham, renting herself another cheap room above a bar in which she had found work, not twenty miles from his home. Camden had a devil of a time hiding her correspondence from Veronica, an easier time excusing his frequent trips to San Francisco to perpetuate the illicit affair.

As the affair graduated from exotic to routine, the demands began, and Camden suddenly found himself struggling to balance a shrewish, depressed wife, who began to resent his absences, and a calculating, occasionally violent mistress, who wanted him to marry her, and threatened to expose him as a philanderer if he refused. So, he agreed, ousting Veronica on the grounds that she had ceased to interest him. For her part, she seemed relieved to be freed of him, even more so when her terms of alimony were accepted.

Bronwyn moved in two weeks after Veronica's departure, and immediately Camden knew he had made a mistake, not in forcing Veronica out, but in letting Bronwyn in. For as boring as he had grown to find his first wife, she had at least kept to herself and her only outbursts seemed to originate from her desire to have the life he'd given her but with someone else in his place. Bronwyn, on the other hand, was moody almost incessantly and frequently lashed out at him for violations both real and imagined. Despite the facts surrounding her usurpation of Veronica's position in Camden House, she constantly questioned his comings and goings, and went through his correspondence with all the diligence of Sherlock Holmes. And when she found confirmation of her suspicions, as she was eventually bound to, her reaction was not with a sharp tongue, but a loaded gun, and her response to his admission of guilt was to lodge a bullet in his spine, robbing him of the use of his legs.

Bronwyn's arrest and subsequent imprisonment, however, meant the situation in which he now found himself could not be her doing, unless she had agents abroad who were committed to doing her bidding. And he found it hard to believe she could inspire loyalty in anyone from behind bars.

In the weeks after the news broke, Veronica had resurfaced, offering to take care of his every need, if he'd only take her back. He had refused, and when next he heard from her, it was a letter announcing her intent to take her own life if she didn't hear from him within the month. That was on April 8th. Preoccupied with his own suffering, and unwilling to let it coerce him into repeating past mistakes, he ignored the letter.

On March 1st, Veronica was found hanging naked by her neck from the rafters of a bedroom she'd shared with a known criminal and opium addict, Gerald Higgins. Higgins was never heard from again, but reliable word said he had fled and was now somewhere in Canada, fixing shoes for a living.

Which left him with no one, for none of the women had borne him any children who might have grown into ill-fitting shoes of vengeance, nor had he wished for them.

The air was getting thin. Camden raised a hand and scratched his fingernails against the lid of the coffin. He was not yet afraid, for he didn't fear death, nor did he believe that was the motive behind his internment. A murderer does not leave a bell with which to signal the watchmen or the lantern to enable detection of the rope. This was a message, the first stage of a plan that would end in a demand for exorbitant sums of money unless he wanted to be buried for good.

Another scratch against the wood, and Camden froze.

He looked at his fingers, hovering just beneath the coffin lid. He had been in the process of lowering his hand when he'd heard the sound.

On the other side of the wood, on the *outside*, something scratched again.

A small rain of dirt hissed through the fissure above his feet.

For a moment he considered that the sound might possibly be that of a shovel cleaving through the dirt as his antagonist dug him up. Which would mean Camden's refusal to ring the bell which had been provided for him had had the desired effect. They had buried him, given him the lamp and the rope, and hoped he would awaken in panic. They would have expected the bell to start clang-clanging away moments after he regained consciousness. His silence would have confused them, and doubt would have followed. After all, there was any number of ways he could die down here: suffocation or intoxication by the lantern smoke; he could be burned alive if the lantern tipped over; or, if he suffered from claustrophobia, he might wake up only to die of fright, his heart exploding from the panic. And if they wanted his money, they couldn't take that chance.

Another scratch, and the image of the shovel evaporated. The sound was too quick, too furtive to be that of anything but a scavenger, this one motivated by no riches other than the succulent bounty lying hidden beyond the walls of the human body.

A rat.

The graveyard would be awash with them, and at the sound of this one's urgency, others would come.

Another drizzle of dirt and Camden coughed again. Tears leaked from his eyes. The lamp's flame was guttering, the shadows thrashing against the pine walls of the coffin as the smoke began to mute the light.

Perhaps he had let them wait long enough, after all. His lungs were beginning to burn, his throat closing against the poisoned air. He imagined once they released him, it would take him quite a while before he would be able to do anything but hack forth the vile black sludge he'd ingested during his incarceration.

While fumbling for the bell cord, he grazed the flesh of his hand against a nail that had been driven into the right wall of the coffin. The cord nudged his wrist. Camden hesitated, blinked away the hot tears stinging his eyes and noticed that the nail was not just the result of shoddy, hasty workmanship. It was keeping something pinned there. Something he had missed until now because of the thickening smoke and because the paper was only a shade darker than the wood to which it had been affixed. Also, he hadn't really been looking for correspondence from his captor when their intent had appeared to be obvious. *Take time to think about your situation, and when you're ready to meet our demands, ring the bell.*

With one hand, he snatched the note free, tearing the blank space at the top. The other, he used to sleeve away the moisture from his burning eyes. Then he brought the note up close to his face and began to read. The words were hard to make out at first, but when eventually he pieced them together, he let the paper fall to his chest and lay as still as the corpse he would soon become.

His body went numb.

Above his head, more scratching.

The coffin filled with smoke, and the flame went out.

Darkness.

As the words echoed over and over and over again in his head, the old man tried to draw in enough breath to scream in the oily dark but could only half fill his lungs before he began to cough and choke and splutter.

He reached blindly for the bell, despite knowing now that there was no use and yet needing so desperately to believe he hadn't been such a fool. When he found it, he tugged and tugged and tugged again until the cord broke and fell to coil around his limp fingers like a dead snake.

Up there in the autumnal graveyard, he knew, were watchmen. But they would have heard nothing, for there was nothing to hear but the skittering of dead leaves across silent graves. But perhaps, if they were close, they might yet hear him scream, if he could only find the air.

A loud crack and he heard the earth began to pour into the lower end of the coffin.

Soon, the rats would follow.

Weeping, Camden touched the note, at the words written there by the fair hand of his long-lost Rebecca, who, he now realized, he had never really known at all. How, he wondered in his panic, had he so misinterpreted her cunning, her callousness, her hatred of him? How had he not realized that what he had done to her father would leave no room or capability for affection? A lifetime of studying adversaries had left him blind to the enemy within his own chambers. Rebecca, whom he had ample cause to love, if only he'd been able. Now, he wondered if that inability had been caused by some subconscious recognition of her true nature.

Rebecca.

Because she had appeared to love him, and because she had asked for nothing, he had left her everything. Thus, fulfilling her plan all along.

He closed his eyes, the smoke too much to bear, and put a hand over his mouth, a redundant gesture meant to prolong a life already over.

The note, the note. It may as well have been painted behind his eyelids for all the peace it gave him.

*Why?* he asked himself, but that question and all others, had already been answered.

The note, the note. A simple poem, written in her loving hand:

*I can feel you smiling and ever so sure, though you're buried underground*
*Content to play at being dead, dependent on a sound*
*But salvation from god, nor human hand, shall ever for you come*
*And ample time you'll have down there, to ponder all you've done*

As he began to convulse, Camden reached a trembling hand up and out to what he'd thought was a nail driven into the coffin wall. And though he could feel his strength beginning to fade as the first of the rats thumped with a squeal to the floor of the coffin and the smoke filled him with darkness, he managed to work it free.

It was too smooth to be a nail. Too heavy. And rounded at one end.

*You stole my father's livelihood; took my mother's health*
*So I'll think of you and smile as I spend your hard-earned wealth*
*I am leaving you to die where the dark doth know you well*
*And consider a debt repaid, while you burn in the fires of Hell.*

Despite the agony, the torment, the panic that came with being unable to draw a breath, Camden could not help but grin as the life left him and more rats began to wriggle into his coffin. He could not feel them as they hit his useless legs, but he could feel the vibrations through his body.

He turned the smooth object over in his fingers before letting it drop the floor.

*Foolish old man.*

He had led a life of conquering that would make Napoleon proud. He had been merciless, undone only by the occasional foolish notion, and even then, he had restricted such lapses to matters of romance, never business. And they had come together to destroy him anyway. Losing the use of his legs had not softened him one bit or forced his dismissal from the game of chess that was his life, a game in which he had always considered himself one step ahead of the competition.

And in the end, he had been foolish enough to gamble everything on a simple little bell, the tolling of which would free him to better evaluate the situation so that he could dominate it and emerge the victor once more. A bell from which the clapper had been removed, muting it. Rebecca, knowing him perhaps better than he ever had, or ever would, know himself, had used it to nail the note to the wall.

And when the smoke, the earth and the rats descended upon him in one cracking, roaring, screeching mass, he had time for one final epiphany.

If he had never quite loved Rebecca, he certainly did now.

For she was nothing less than his equal.

# WILL YOU TELL THEM I DIED QUIETLY?

I TRIED TO BE LIKE THEM ONCE. *I tried to stop. It didn't work. Couldn't work after your uncle brought The Yawning Thing home. That made it worse. That brought the dreams, and the dreams said I should die and die quietly. For this, I need your help. Will you help me?*

Yes, if you promise not to hate me.

*Of course. I could never hate you, nor should you ever hate me. Not for this. Hate them instead. All of them.*

The shrieking of tires further down the rain-slicked road made Elias jump. Concerned, his uncle clamped a hand on his shoulder. "Okay?" he asked, and Elias nodded, then looked up at the roiling quicksilver sky. It had been raining since her death. Endless rain that turned the earth to sludge and darkened moods already somber. He gritted his teeth until they hurt and let his uncle steer him into the crowd of walking umbrellas clustered at the churchyard gates. Autumn hissed past them clinging wetly to the wheels of a hurried driver and the stooped men hunched further away from the icy spray.

The graveyard yawned wide revealing crooked stone teeth set on green-capped gums of misshapen earth. They would put her somewhere hidden, in a plot no one else wanted, Elias knew. Somewhere she wouldn't be found unless by chance or mistake. In the weeds, perhaps, for their generosity could only extend so far after all these years spent hating.

Somewhere quiet.

He watched black heels creating echoes on the paved path, stared at the stockinged feet of their owners and felt the anger flare once more, searing the inside of his cold skin, heating his cheeks.

He watched the congregation of strangers, bustling purposefully forward through the sheets of rain; unfamiliar shapes garbed in misery they would cast off once they had muttered the words expected of them. All niceties spun from the remnants of old hatred.

This was a soulless, senseless, unhallowed place where the ground prospered on the bones of more strangers. No one mattered here, neither the living nor the dead.

He was already starting to regret agreeing to let them take her here.

A tall thin figure with a shredded cloud for hair parted the crowd and floated through the gray towards them. Elias sighed to a halt, accepted the squeeze of his uncle's hand again and nodded. Reverend Flood mimicked it, disrupted the carefully placed creases in his face with a practiced smile.

"Elias." For a moment nothing but a sad, slow shake of his head. "I'm so glad you decided to let us perform the ceremony. In times like these it is of no use to anyone to keep old feuds going, wouldn't you agree?"

Elias frowned, tautened the silence between them with a glare at the holy man, bore his uncle's attempt at a thank you and let himself be ferried further toward the grave. Inside, his guts rolled coldly. *Feuds?* Is that what they called it? Or had he missed a note of mockery in the reverend's words? His face reddened. Then he thought of Veronica. She would have laughed, and that made the first smile of the day corkscrew the corners of his mouth.

The shadow of the church dropped over them, steam rising from the skin of a crowd that had unified to become a solid, shifting mass of hushed tones and clucked sympathetic tongues. Elias hated them then, wanted to hurt them, to shriek his rage at them, to scare them into revealing the true purpose for their presence here. But instead he said nothing and let the memory of Veronica's patience carry him beneath a steeple pretending to fall in time with their advance. The wind hurried them; the rain needled them, and they were inside, awash in the warmth of an alleged grace and a phalanx of candles. Heads turned; white smudges draped in hollow pockets of mourning watching for victims, perfecting solemnity.

And it was quiet.

"You should probably sit up front," his uncle said and at last his hand was removed. "She would have wanted you to."

Elias moved away from him, sparing him a glance as he did so. Uncle Travis had never been close; was no closer now despite his valiant attempts to be supportive. He had in fact been relegated to little more than a blurry figure in the background of his mother's photos and his nephew's recollections from years past. The smile he offered Elias was tired and confused. He was just as out of place as his nephew, but less equipped to deal with it. The old man lowered his painfully thin frame into a seat, next to a withered old woman whose one good eye rolled to watch him.

The carpet in the aisle was red velvet and whispered against the soles of Elias's shoes. He noticed black crescent symbols—meaningless to anyone not well versed in the way of the New World—slipping beneath his feet. Then gone. He raised his head. The altar was a morgue slab dressed in veils that clung greedily to the shadows of the candles. Behind it, set high in the old stone wall an orb of stained glass rose, a kaleidoscope of ill-formed images, fragmented faces with jigsaw skin, all bowed in supplication to some higher power Elias didn't care to know. He was not here to give thanks.

*Will you tell them? Will you expose their narrow-minded ways and tell them I died because of this? Because of the Yawning Thing? It stands there, wanting me to be inside it you know, wanting me to become one with it. Such a terrible graceless thing.*

At the head of the church sat a rigid cabal of imposters. To Elias, they were as loathsome as the black-clad throng who'd crawled through the churchyard like starving cats. For a moment they made no move to make room for him, but eventually a sneer was cast his way and they swept aside on a wave of grumbled whispers. He sat and ignored the fetid stench radiating from the fraternity. Sat and waited.

The candles flickered.

Reverend Flood drifted from within the ill-lit recesses, through the gloom into the fluttering light, his eyes wide and flitting from face to face. His spotless black shoes made no sound on the marble steps as he ascended the altar from the left, genuflected, and floated into position behind the slab, head bowed. Elias felt his skin ripple and tears of anger fill his eyes. *I should not have let them take her*, he thought and was answered by her voice: *There is no shame in lying with the enemy if the enemy is not aware of itself.* He nodded to himself, shuddered off the lingering skeins of repulsion at being so close, so caught inside a crowd of his family's one-time persecutors and listened.

*I'm fading. Are you there? Tell me you won't leave. I'm scared. See how it watches me? See how it wants me?*

Don't be frightened. I won't leave.

*Will you tell them I died quietly?*

Yes.

*Even if I don't?*

What? What does that mean? You said—

*I'm fading. Quick, grab the needle...*

"We are gathered here to pay our respects to a most unique and curious woman. A woman misunderstood by many. A woman who suffered under the terms of old superstitions, stubbornly upheld by the ill-educated among our parish. It is time we put an end to such nonsense once and for all." Though swathed in cloaks hewn to imbue divinity, the elderly reverend wore one too many shadows, his face one too many lines for Elias to believe him sincere. The charitable words fell from his mouth like worms from a fallen pail. As if he'd read the thought, the holy man fixed him with a hard stare, a half-smile dancing on his thin lips.

"Grief unites us all, my friends, regardless of our religion and in grief, people can be saved."

Rain thudded dully against a roof so high above them it could not be seen in the gloom.

Smoke ghosts wrenched themselves away from the candles as the front doors were heaved closed.

"Let us pray for her immortal soul," Flood commanded. "Pray for the soul of Veronica Ryman, that her body may rest, and her soul find peace in the afterlife." The sudden silence prompted by the reverend's words brought a startling and impossibly obvious question hammering into the forefront of Elias's mind.

The body.

*Where is her body? It should be here.*

It was a burial. He had assumed the coffin would take its place at the head of the church. Had he misinterpreted the rituals of these common folk?

He stood and dragged the upset murmurs of the crowd up by his elbows. For the first time he noticed the thrumming, as of an engine buried beneath the church. His blood vibrated with it as around him, shadowed heads nodded in glee at his confusion. Sudden, almost debilitating fury struck him, flooding his veins with adrenaline, drowning the fear that lapped at his throat. Then he was up and out and stalking towards the altar, where the reverend's arms were held aloft as if expecting his faith to keep the roof above their heads should it deign to fall.

Elias clenched his fists to his sides and mounted the steps; cast a venomous glance at the holy man before he turned to face the congregation.

Towards the back of the church and the shadows gathered there, his uncle's hand waved objection, little more than a pale shape shifting in the gloom. He ignored it.

Thunder grumbled over their heads. Murmurs leaked from the pews and gathered in pools of dissension in the aisle.

*I loved her*, Elias realized. *This would never have happened if I had told her so, given her hope. Something else to think about besides that* thing.

"Son," said Reverend Flood, the abstract flow of his garments belying the benevolent composure on his fissured face. "I understand you're upset."

"Do you?" Elias said with a bitter grin. "Perhaps I'd be less upset if you'd tell me where she is."

"What? Where who is? You mean your mother?"

"Who else are you burying today?"

Shock snapped the spines of those who'd been content to bow their heads and ignore the proceedings and now all faces were raised and staring.

Flood shook his head, brow furrowed. "She's here. We'll bury her after the ceremony, like we always do. Why are you so upset?"

"Why isn't she here in the church? Is that part of your goddamned ritual? I want to know where she is. Now."

Flood leaned closer and Elias had to struggle not to back up a step. A hush rushed from the back of the church through the pews and swept against his cheek like a blow that had fallen short. There came what might have been a muffled cry of pain and he looked out at the crowd. Silent, somber faces. His uncle's hand still raised and waving.

"Would you have preferred she be displayed, Elias," Flood whispered. "In the condition you left her in?"

Elias felt his rage surge inside him. Lies wept from the open wound of the holy man's mouth, sickening him. "You said she'd be treated like anyone else," he said through clenched teeth. "Why isn't her body in the church?"

Flood looked evenly at him. "Who said it isn't?"

"Then where is her coffin?"

Incense filled the air, though Elias had seen none burning. Silence stretched out between them as it had in the churchyard before his uncle had bade him move on.

A mistake.

This was all a mistake.

He was seeing the truth now as if the opacity of their false promises had been ripped from his eyes. Elias and his family were pariahs. His mother's death should have been a triumph for them. Instead they had offered to inter her on their ground, by way of a peace offering. But what holy man would voluntarily offer to give peace and eternal life to a witch?

Elias had swallowed the hurt, the pain, the grief at her passing, had weathered their choreographed mourning despite the clear memory of their cruelty to her while she lived. He had walked among them, bristling with repulsion at the mere thought of being so close, nauseated by his willingness to accept their pitiful gestures of condolence. No longer. The charade would end one way or another. He would tear the façade down around them, then take her body away and bury her where she would have wished.

"Son," said Flood, "you didn't bring her to us in a coffin."

*They called it* Nocturnity, *Elias. Though on the placard at its feet it says* The Yawning Thing. *It was supposed to be a symbol of sleep, a cure for insomniacs who were instructed down through the ages to gaze upon it so that it might make them tired by looking at another man's exhausted image. It didn't though. It drove them mad, sent them into fevers, bestowed night terrors upon them, haunted them until they splintered their own bones and split their skins trying to climb inside its mouth. Your father brought it to me. Said it would look after me, help me to sleep while he was off on another of his acquisitions trips. It didn't though, and he never returned. Since then, it has stood right where it is now, watching me, whispering perverse things to me in the twilight between sleep and wakefulness, telling me to die quietly before it consumes me whole. And I believe it. Don't you?*

I don't know.

*Of course you do. You're such a good boy and you must help me. You must save me from it. You must ensure that I cannot see it, that I am not here to bear witness to it when it comes to tear me asunder.*

But how?

*You'll know.*

"You murdered her," Elias said and sneered into the reverend's face. "If not for you she'd have been able to run, to get help. All of you killed her." He pointed out at the crowd and his breath caught, his finger fell. The congregation was standing, a black sea of motionless figures, faces raised and twisted in the candlelight. Watching him. Something scraped against a wall near the back of the church.

"It was you who did the murdering," Flood told him. "You and your kind."

The rain thundered overhead; the floor hummed underfoot.

Elias stared, felt the weight of the congregation at his back. "I helped her. I gave her a quiet death."

Flood gave a sad smile. "I'm afraid not," he said. "I'm afraid it wasn't that quiet at all and you know it."

*I can see him, Elias. I can still see him watching. Take my eyes. Take that needle. Take them. I don't want to see it anymore. Make me blind to it. Quick, quick. Good boy. Oh God...*

83

"It's why you brought the statue," Flood continued. "It's why you agreed to let us have her. You thought she'd gone crazy, and she had. What you didn't know was that she was right." He nodded toward the sacristy, where beside a small stained-glass door, the shadows were thick. Elias followed his gaze. "Is-is she there?"

"God gives the power to those who know how to control it, my son. The statue was meant to find us. There is no room left for your kind."

Elias wasn't listening. His feet had found the steps. The doors at the front of the church rattled. He looked in that direction, saw his uncle still waving, though now his hand was free of his body and being held aloft by a stranger.

Trapped.

They'd walked right into it. It hurt his head to think about how long the machinery must had been turning to bring them here, to bring down his family, his mother. Panic seized him, siphoned the air from his lungs and he gasped and tumbled forward into the gloom. *At least she's here*, he thought frantically. *I'll see her one last time.* He could ask her forgiveness for not ushering her out as he was supposed to, for making her death anything but quiet. She had died with a guttural scream he'd had to sever with a carving knife, the horror tattooed on her face as she choked on her own blood. No. Not quiet.

He flung himself deeper into the gloom, his fumbling hands warmed by feverish breath he prayed was his own. The thrumming in the floor felt almost pleasurable now, sending a tingling up through the soles of his feet. Feeble light strained through the stained-glass door of the sacristy. Beyond it figures moved, their arms dwindling into curved, raised shapes. Sharper shadows. He ignored them, continued to search the corner, met the mottled stone of the wall, kicked against the rug when it gathered like a tired dog at his feet and then...

*Here.*

Cold, polished marble slipped beneath his fingertips.

*Nocturnity. The Yawning Thing.*

Behind him the carpet whispered to him of the advance of the throng.

"Forgive me," he said as a break in the crowd revealed the face of the statue. A long thin face with wide eyes and an impossibly long mouth looked back at him. Black marble. From between its teeth, bloodstained blonde hair trailed down to its muscular, lifeless chest. Elias closed his eyes, sank heavily to his knees. "She didn't die quietly," was all he could think to say as the congregation drew a tight circle around him and hissed curses down on his head.

As one, the candles went out.

A final breeze touched his face and he smiled, imagined it was her fingertips brushing his lips.

"Neither will you," someone said as the curved shadows descended from over their heads.

# THE TRADITION

**Y**OU'RE ALONE.

She awoke, slowly, blinking to rid the darkness from her eyes, but it refused to leave. Instead it separated like a tattered curtain through which hung only feeble strains of light. It was dark, much darker than she liked, and it had been that way for as long as she'd been here, sitting on the stairs, waiting with the smell of mildew and dust in her nose.

*What are you waiting for, Evelyn?*

She frowned at the question, knowing the answer was there, hiding perhaps between those gently shifting veils of lighter dark, but it would not come. There was a purpose for her presence here. Of course there was. Perhaps it was only the muddle-headedness of lingering sleep that kept it from her, or perhaps it was not a purpose she wished to embrace. Perhaps she was here because it was a hiding place. But if so, from whom or what had she been hiding.

She forced a smile.

*You're being silly.*

Yes, most likely that was all. After all, hadn't Chad always said—?

*Chad!* She seized on the name like a swimmer clutching a lifeline, and for a moment his face resolved itself from the gloom before her—a pale oblong briefly illuminated by cold light from a distant moon through rents in the rotten roof above. Then it was gone, scattered like dandelion seeds on an unfelt breath. She watched them drift away until they were swallowed by the shadows stretched across the debris-laden hallway floor.

Upstairs, a soft groan as the floorboards in a deserted room recalled the passage of a long-dead tenant. Then once more, the house remembered quiet.

Alone in an empty house, with nothing but the night and the solitary blade of blue moonlight that, freed of a cloud, sliced its way through the hole in the roof above her head, narrowly missing her slender arm, Evelyn sighed.

Although she was not afraid of where she had found herself, she was afraid she would never remember why and so be forced to remain here playing at being a ghost while her stricken mind struggled to remember...*why?* Why was she here? Had she fallen while exploring, perhaps striking her head in the very place that retained the memory of such intrusions? Gingerly, she probed the back of her skull and found only cobwebs, dirt, and what felt like the spine of an old dead leaf, which she plucked free and tossed away. There was no pain, no bruises, no dried blood, and now that consciousness had had time to return in full, no disorientation but for the obvious gaping hole in her recollection.

Lack of any apparent motivation for her ending up in such a curious place led her to consider briefly the possibility that it was all a dream, albeit an odd one in which she apparently had little to do.

*Do I know this place?* she wondered and peered at her surroundings in the gloom.

Most of the stair steps were broken, the old red carpet that had once lent it a regal aspect now shredded, worn, and in places, torn away. Leading away from the stairs, slivers of old marble tile could still be glimpsed beneath a chaos of plaster, broken furniture and the remains of an old chandelier. Through the resulting hole in the hallway ceiling, she could see straight up through the jagged teeth of broken floorboards to the room above and beyond its own shattered ceiling to the night sky, speckled with straining stars washed out by the moon. Strands of ivy hung down from the hole like hangman's ropes.

The main door of the house had once held glass in the upper half of the frame, but that was long gone, as were the boards that had been nailed to fill the hole.

Evelyn stood, tired of waiting for memory to catch up, and turned, the stairs creaking under her feet. At the top of the stairs, where the moon could not reach, the darkness was thick and unwelcoming, but Evelyn reasoned that if anything here meant her harm, it could have satisfied its need while she'd slept.

She moved up the stairs, carefully avoiding broken bottles and syringes left here by teenagers seeking a haven in which to become acquainted with Hell and reached the landing. The hallway ahead was narrow, flanked by doorways in which the doors themselves had been removed, sold perhaps as antiquities to grace the jambs of newer places.

In one of the bedrooms lay a soiled mattress, sagging in the middle from the weight of heaving young bodies, the homeless, and the rain.

In another, a bureau had been relieved of its drawers, and the glass from its oval mirror, though some enterprising soul had collected the fragments of the latter, and, together with multicolored pieces of glass from shattered beer bottles, used them to fashion a curious and senseless mural of slivers on the opposite wall. The resulting creation looked like a symbol of destruction.

She moved on.

The bathroom had been consumed by moss and mold, the tiles lost beneath a green skin, the tub overturned, claw feet pawing stiffly at the air.

In what appeared to be a child's bedroom, she stopped.

Intruders had defiled the room. It reeked of them, had their signatures on the wall in large dripping letters. In a splintered cradle to the left of a shard of moonlight, a doll had been painted to look like a whore. One of its eyes had been removed and replaced with a bottle cap stuffed without care into the rubber socket. Condoms were scattered like shed snake skins among stacks of old newspapers, empty bottles, and soiled, crumpled up sleeping bags.

The sudden and unexpected offense she took at the disrespect these interlopers had shown to the memory of whoever had once called this place home forced her to question any ties she might have had to them.

Had she once lived here?

Or—a less pleasant thought—had she *been* one of the defilers, perhaps the conscientious one, vainly trying to persuade her friends not to do what they had in mind, but helpless to do anything but play along when they ignored her?

If that were true, it suited her to think that she might have been the sole voice of reason, the good apple among the bad. But why should that be any more of a plausible possibility than any other?

Somewhere in the shadows of the room, a child began to sing.

Evelyn's breath caught, and she took an involuntary step back, a hand to her chest.

She listened.

The singing was soft, faint, and not at all sad. Instead it was a cheerful, festive song, perhaps even with a trace of mischief, a song that could only be created by children in defiance of authority, and only heard in the absence of that authority.

Evelyn cocked her head.

"Everything's dark, nothing is bright," the child sang, "No one can stop us on Halloween night."

Evelyn smiled.

"This is our night, this is our street, give us some money, or candy to eat."

The singing grew louder, and now Evelyn realized it was not coming from the room at all. It drifted through the empty window frame and over the sill from somewhere on the street outside.

Children were coming.

A firefly of excitement dispelled the suffocating gloom within her, and she started back toward the stairs.

The skin of the house settled onto its skeleton as she walked, and abruptly, as if waiting for her to stop trying so hard, she remembered something, and the firefly became a swarm that lit her from the inside out.

She had not come here alone. There had been others.

There had been a joke. No, not a joke exactly. A game. Chad and—what was her name?—Jessica! Yes, that was it. Chad and Jessica, and someone else whose name she could not recall but had faith that like the others it would come in time. A game, the rules of which eluded her for now, but there had been laughter and singing and she had not been alone. Remembering this much made her vigil more bearable. Yes, they had brought her here and left her alone, but they would be back. That, she suspected, had been part of the game. A dare, perhaps. Stay a while in the scary house on...

She closed her eyes, saw still frame pictures of leaf-lined streets, damp pavements, cars with autumn leaves snagged in their windshield wipers...

Seldom Seen Road.

She felt tension drain from her shoulders she hadn't realized was there. Sighed, wished she had a cigarette or perhaps a magazine, something to do to kill the time.

A game. A dare.

*Trick-or-treat.*

Yes, pebbles in a drainpipe. The answers were coming, the memories falling to land behind her eyes. Slowly, so slowly, but they were there. She was the bait, the lure for the children who looked upon this old, rotting house as a plaything, a catalyst for false fear they would giggle about later with sticky fingers and chocolate teeth as they sat bathed together in the blue light from their television spook shows. Yes. A joke. Nothing more.

Chad, and Jessica, and...Alex! She could almost see them, hear them. Good friends, close friends, *loving* friends who had nominated *her* to be the ghost this year.

Ah yes...The Tradition.

Every year. Every Halloween. But who was it last year? She smiled; it faded fast. Who was it last year? She was afraid to think for too long lest she discover she was the bait then too, or force remembrance back into the recesses of her mind.

Who...?

No, there had been others.

Scare the children but reward their fear.

*Give them some-thing good to eat*, she thought in a sing-song voice.

She bit her lip, felt it bleed, and winced.

*I don't have any candy.*

*Something pretty then.*

She hurried back to the room with the ruined bureau.

The singing grew louder.

"Want to be dared, want to be chased..."

She plucked the glass mosaic from the wall, startled by sudden sobs as they dug under her fingernails.

"Be sure to stay away from the girl with glass in her face."

She froze as the singing died on the breeze, the last of the words lingering like a held breath in the empty hallways.

Chad and Jessica, and Alex. Close friends, dear friends. And she was right, she realized as more of the glass came away, as one of her nails lifted off and fell with a tiny sound to the floor, she *had* been the sole voice of reason.

She had begged them not to bring her here.

She had begged them not to leave her here.

Bleeding.

The remains of the mosaic shimmered through the tears. Panic and hurt doused the fire, leaving only fat rotten flies buzzing lazily around her stomach.

They had hurt her.

Slowly she moved to the stairs, the glass digging into her hands, jutting from beneath the few nails that remained, pricking her lips from where Chad had, after taking her by force, driven shards of his broken beer bottle up into her gums because she wouldn't stop screaming.

Her sobs became a wail. She staggered on the steps. Some of the glass fell as she sagged against the wall.

"Oh God," she whispered.

Movement downstairs distracted her, and she looked up, cleared her vision with her hands, forgetting the glass she still held, uncaring when the shards tore across eyes that had not needed to see for exactly eleven years.

A shadow appeared in the front door. The leaves of an overgrown bush hissed and scraped against the crumpled siding. The shadow moved on. A child whispered fearfully, then was silent.

Alone.

Evelyn listened, then allowed herself a smile, allowed it to warm her away the chill.

It was perfectly natural to forget, she told herself. They had hurt her, betrayed her, but still, still somehow, she had loved them, perhaps because she had never believed that they would allow her into their circle. She knew she would do whatever they asked of her, within reason, and even through the corruption into which they had led her, she steadfastly clung to everything that had made her who she was.

And here, despite the anguish, or perhaps because of it, in the house on Seldom Seen Road, she was whole again, waiting for them to come back.

She descended the steps, pausing midway down to inspect the glimmer of light on her wrist. The moonlight illuminated her bracelet and her smile grew. Silver snakes biting each other's tails as they chased a pearl. She did not need to remove the trinket to know what the inscription on the back said. It was a proclamation of adoration and acceptance by people she had envied and worshiped and longed for so many nights when she had had no one.

Friends forever.

She shuddered with delight, her ankle snapping as she shifted stance, and she winced. It had sounded like a branch breaking and would surely give her away if the children heard. The nature of the game was of course to stay quiet, to stay invisible until they came, singing and whispering and daring each other to brave the cavernous husk of a house no more haunted than their bedroom closets.

Quiet.

She waited.

In the moonlight, the dust danced. Excitement coursed through her at the sight of three new shadows growing long in the doorway as she watched. In the dark it was easy to imagine terrible things. In the dark it was easy to be afraid, to draw ghosts from listing doors and gaping floors but hadn't they chosen her for her imperviousness to such foolishness? Of course they had. They had laughed and clapped and devised this chilling plan for the children in the feeble light of the October dusk and she had known then it would be unnerving but had known too she could bear it. After all those years of solitude, of social ineptitude, there was nothing left that could frighten her.

But how thrilling the idea of frightening them, returned all these years later to see if she abided by the rules, even when they had taken it upon themselves to change them.

The memory of the blood from her hands pattered on the steps, disappeared when they struck.

"C'mon," someone whispered, and she watched him move into the doorway, nothing but a moving patch of tar untouched by the scythe of blue light above his head. "What's taking so long?"

Evelyn froze, afraid to breathe. She must wait until the right moment and prayed she would know it when it came.

Another shape crept into the hall, following the first. "Jesus, I can't believe we're doing this."

A boy and a girl.

*Chad, Jessica...*

"Now that we're here you want to leave? You kidding me?"

"Let's just go back to the party."

"Fuck that. Besides, I want to see her."

The girl stopped moving. "It's just an old house. There's no her to see."

"If she's a myth, then why are you afraid?"

"I'm not afraid, this is just dumb, that's all. Probably get a lung disease from all the crap floating in the air."

A third figure entered the room. "Fuck, it stinks in here."

"The hell kept you so long, we thought y—"

Evelyn moved, just a little, but the step creaked, and the shadows looked up. She willed herself to be invisible, just as she had through her torturous teens when the good-looking boys and the beautiful popular girls had come her way, just as she had when her mother burnt her with cigarettes for having her no-good father's eyes. Just as she had when she'd cut herself and the other girls had wanted to see so they had another reason to think she was a freak.

Invisible. It used to be so easy. She closed her eyes and hugged herself tight, her glass-shard teeth sinking into her lower lip: *Please don't let them see me. Please don't let them see me...Please...*

A hushed whisper. "Did you hear that?"

"It was just the stairs creaking. Don't you freak out on me too, man."

The girl: "I didn't freak out, asshole."

"Whatever. Let's just see what there is to see and then we can go get toasted at Joy's place."

In the swollen darkness, Evelyn smiled. They hadn't seen her. She had maintained the suspense, and wouldn't they be so surprised to see that she had waited for them all these years. She listened, could taste the fear in them. Did they expect she'd be angry, still?

No, she wasn't angry. Could never be angry at the only people who had ever loved her.

With a sigh, she stood and raised her fingers so that the moonlight found them.

She just didn't want to be alone anymore.

"Hey, Rick...Hey, shit! *What is that?*"

She descended with deliberate drama, drawing on all the horror movies she had ever seen, locked in her bedroom all those many dark and dreary nights. The memories were there, cavorting with gleeful abandon behind her eyes.

"What are you talking about, Stan? I don't see anything!"

*I see you. They see me. All I want is love.*

"Rick, I mean it...what *is* that? Look, on the stairs, there's something there!"

Evelyn began to hum the song she had heard them sing. The song of the splinter girl she had once found cruel, but now knew was their way of immortalizing her, of rejoicing in the person, the woman, she had become.

"It's a joke, it's Mike...it has to be. Jesus..."

In an instant she was at the foot of the stairs and smiling. They smiled back for a moment and then their harlequin faces slid back to reveal the unsmiling terror-stricken faces beneath. They did not look the same, but then she could hardly recall what they had looked like all those years ago. They hadn't grown older, but neither had she.

She felt the dust shift around her as they drew in breath to power their screams, to unleash the chorus that would spoil the game.

*Love me again,* she whispered and rushed forward through the moonlight to embrace them.

And there were no screams at all as she held them tight, tighter still, the splinters finding their hearts, the moonlight finding their eyes, as Evelyn wept and sang and rejoiced in their reunion.

*Friends forever.*

# THE ONE NIGHT OF THE YEAR

I T'S CLOSE TO MIDNIGHT. The old farmhouse around him expands and contracts like a living, breathing thing as he takes his place on a rickety chair before its dark open mouth. The wood creaks as he settles his old bones, the barrel of the shotgun cold through the knees of his jeans. Beside him on the porch, faithful as always, sits Rufus, his salt-and-pepper Jack Russell terrier. He is sitting up, ears pricked, eyes fixed on the dark cornfield that hushes and sways in the wind thirty feet from the front of the house.

Only the porchlight is on. Caleb has extinguished all other lights inside the house. There's nobody else inside so the dark won't bother anyone. There hasn't been anyone else inside that house for nigh-on a decade now. The porch light is the only one he needs tonight anyway. When they come out of the corn, they'll come close enough for him to see their faces.

Rufus growls low in his throat. Caleb reaches down and ruffles the back of his neck. "It's okay, boy," he says, and the dog whines and falls silent.

The corn continues to hiss and sway, a pale ocean out there in the gloom, hiding a universe worth of life from his ageing eyes.

The silver coin of the moon slips from the pocket of the clouds and turns the night monochrome. A chill breeze sends dead leaves skittering toward the porch. Rufus shivers, ducks his head as if cowed by the ease with which the night can turn unkind.

Balancing the shotgun across his knees, Caleb fishes from his shirt pocket a pack of Winstons. He offers one to the dog, who spares him only the briefest of glances before resuming his vigilant watch on the cornfield. With a slight grin, Caleb withdraws the offer and pokes a cigarette into his mouth, lights it, enjoying the sulfuric scent of the match, the sudden flare of warm light, before all that is left is the gloom and the heat of the smoke in his lungs. He tosses the match out onto the dirt between the porch and the cornfield. Around him, the house groans.

Caleb exhales the smoke into the air, watches the breeze whip it into frenzied ghosts, and closes his eyes. He is getting old, too old to sustain the kinds of memories that once kept him afloat. His mind has become the house, crumbling, dilapidated, the rooms empty but for fading memories of the life they once contained. All the color has gone, the wallpaper peeling away from the walls, the floorboards covered in dust his arthritic bones won't allow him to clean, even if he was of a mind to. All the rooms are quiet now, and as the days go by and the years slip away, it seems not even his passage through them creates a sound. It's as if his presence was only measurable in the eyes of others, and in their absence, he has become immaterial. Cobwebs make cataracts over the windows, the sills flaking and rotting from within. Dust and dirt clot beneath the furniture. Only the pictures on the mantel have escaped the mildewing of the years, and only those because he tends to them daily.

Rufus growls again, the growl rising to a whine, his flanks shaking from more than just the chill.

"Easy boy." Caleb follows the dogs gaze, but sees nothing but the corn, the stalks hissing as they weave in the breeze. He looks around, but as always, there is nothing but denuded chestnut and walnut trees to the left and right, the house at his back, and the cornfield ahead. And an old man and his dog on the porch.

The dog licks his fingers and he strokes the frightened animal's head.

There will be visitors this night, and both know it, have prepared for it. This past year Caleb has thought of little else. As his mind callously empties itself of his most cherished memories—his dear departed wife's face, his daughter's smile, the color of his son's eyes—there is little else to occupy his time. Instead he wakes, feeds the dog and himself, and eyes the calendar on the wall. Summer, always his favorite time of year, has been reduced now to nothing more than a countdown to fall, to October, and Halloween Night. The night they come to see him.

"And what would we do if they didn't?" he asks aloud. Rufus cocks his head to look at him, but in the absence of any kind of clarity, returns to his watch.

It's a strange question Caleb has asked of himself, but he can't help but ponder it.

The first time they came, seven years ago, he assumed them trick-or-treaters. Sure, it was not usual for them to come this far outside the city limits, and the nearest house was three miles east of here, but that only made their appearance more welcome. Caleb loved Halloween as a child, even as a teen (though his exploits during that period of his life ran to mischief), and as an adult, he had found it easy to be infected by the excitement that filled the house as his children and their mother created elaborate costumes from scratch. He helped carved pumpkins, fill bowls of water with apples for bobbing, played along with their blindfold games, and stayed up late with them to watch old horror movies on their unreliable TV. It was, though he'd never really realized it until now, his favorite time of the year, with Christmas a distant second. Perhaps a childhood spent engrossed in horror comics (*Tales from the Crypt*, *Vault of Fear*, *Eerie*, and the like) had left him more disposed than most men his age to indulge his children in their annual celebration of the macabre. Not only did he tolerate it, he enjoyed it, felt a vicarious thrill as Amanda and Adam cavorted screaming around the farm in their monster costumes. But then his children had grown up and dismissed such childish behavior in favor of real-world pursuits, and now Adam was a doctor in Kenya, Amanda an editor in New York, and his wife Beth was ten years in the grave. In leaving, they had taken the spirit of the season with them, leaving behind a vacant hollow nothing but sadness and loneliness could ever hope to fill. He rarely heard from his children anymore, but as their father, he had little choice but to understand. They had their own lives, their own families, and though he would have liked to hear from them more than once a year, he understood too that wishes were whispers in an awfully loud world.

So, he had grown accustomed to life on the dying farm with only the dog for company, and often that was enough.

And then the visitors had come, their arrival announced by a hysterical volley of barks from Rufus on the porch. Caleb had initially assumed it some night creature having fun tormenting the dog, but when the clamor began to annoy him, his investigation led him outside, where it quickly became evident that he'd been wrong.

Now, beside him, Rufus stands, the hair bristling on his spine, the thought of a bark bubbling in his throat. Caleb shakes off his reverie and sits forward, his hands resting on the stock of the shotgun. The corn continues to weave in the breeze, but now, somewhere in the middle of it, there is a more agitated sound, the *swish swish swish* of passage, the crackle of stalks being trampled underfoot. Clouds cloak the moon, draping a veil of dark over the cornfield. Caleb rises, opens the screen door and fetches an old silver bucket, which he brings with him back to his chair. He sits, slides the bucket between his feet. Rufus takes a moment to sniff at the contents. He is mildly interested, but not enough to abandon his post. Instead he stands at the edge of the porch and begins to bark, his head raised, body tensed and leaning out as if already preparing to run.

Caleb breeches the shotgun, checks that it's loaded, and snaps it shut, finger resting lightly on the trigger as he swings the barrel out, muzzle aimed at the rustling dark.

Abruptly, Rufus ceases his barking. There is silence then but for the breeze. Not even the crickets have much to say this night, muted by the introduction of something unnatural and unknown into their kingdom. Caleb holds his breath, wishing he had a younger man's eyes so that he might have a better chance of picking the visitors out of the gloom.

His heart thunders in his ears, aches in his chest. One of these nights, he knows that ache will become the final toll of the bell and all of this will be over. He wonders if Adam will be able to make the funeral. He wonders if Amanda will weep. In his better hours, more frequent the further from October he gets, he likes to think that his children will miss him and mourn him, that they will not allow the mistakes he has made with them (and there are many) to define their relationship. He hopes they will not forget the good in favor of the bad.

Almost soundlessly, the visitors step from the cornfield.

Caleb feels his body tense, his arthritic fingers stiffening around the stock and barrel of the shotgun.

There are, as always, three of them.

At night, as Caleb lies in bed with Rufus chasing dream rabbits on the floor next to him, he has often wondered if the most obvious and persistent conclusion about the visitors might be the correct one, but forever resists the urge to accept it. To do so would make a horror story of what remains of his life while simultaneously unraveling all the good that's come before. It is an unspeakable thing to consider, and yet it is never so compelling a theory than when he finds himself looking upon them.

Two of them are children, one of them an adult. All of them wear masks that look as if tonight is the only night they are not stored under wet clay. The same could be said for the clothes and the figures who wear them.

*My children*, Caleb thinks, the thought of which he is most afraid. *My wife.*

But of course, this can't be true. Even if he allowed for the supernatural resurrection of his deceased wife, who he steadfastly believes has no reason to haunt him, even if such a thing were possible, his children are still alive. Therefore, it can't be Adam and Amanda dressed in those stained dungarees and rotten pillowcase masks.

They stand shoulder to shoulder before the cornfield, unmoving, silent.

Rufus whines, his occasional bark a strangled sound.

Caleb, eyes fixed on the visitors, reaches into the pail between his feet, and grabs a handful of candy, which he tosses out into the yard. For the longest time, the trick-or-treaters simply stare at him, the eyeholes of the children's pillowcase masks revealing nothing but darkness. Then, with the taller figure looking on, they erupt into fitful giggling and attack the scattered candy, kicking up dirt and squealing in delight as each of them tries to get the lion's share of the fun-sized Mounds, Kit-Kats, Snickers, Milky Ways, and Twixes.

Caleb watches them for a while, but can't keep from staring at the taller figure. Unlike the children, she is not wearing a pillowcase mask. Instead, she wears a pumpkin on her head, a sight he found funny the first time he saw it, until he noticed the candle guttering inside the pumpkin, illuminating the hollowed-out walls, and nothing else. The adult figure does not wear dungarees, rather a filthy nightdress, her small breasts sagging beneath the dirty white material. The nightdress is unfamiliar to Caleb, and for that he is thankful. It assists him in denying the awful possibility that he is looking at his family.

The children finish gathering the candy, their giggles subsiding as, pockets loaded with their bounty, they rejoin the tall figure and all three look at Caleb.

Rufus begins to bark in earnest now, his fear forgotten, or perhaps motivating his protest. He knows what's coming next after all. They both do.

Caleb hoists the shotgun, the barrel resting on one outstretched wrist.

The children stay where they are. The woman, the one he has come to think over the years as The Mother, slowly approaches the porch. She looks from Caleb to the dog, who is frantic now, his outrage and fear echoing around the farm and carrying across the fields.

"Don't," Caleb says.

The Mother ignores him and takes a step toward the dog, her arms coming up as if to embrace him. Or snatch him from the porch.

Caleb pulls the trigger. The shotgun explodes, as does The Mother's head, the pumpkin blown to smithereens, the light extinguished with the life of the thing for whom it was lit. Breathing hard, heart hammering against his ribs, Caleb stands and watches as The Mother staggers back toward her children. They hurry to meet her, their arms extended in assistance, which she accepts. Headless, she falls to her knees, but does not fall, does not die. She never does. As the children fuss and fret over their injured mother, they find the time to look at Caleb where he stands trembling, smoke still trailing from the barrel of the gun.

A quartet of dark eyes study him, but in those elliptical slits, Caleb feels no reproach, no hostility. Instead he feels sadness and pity, and somehow that is so much worse.

"You can't have him," he says, voice quivering. "He's all I've got left."

The pillowcases move as the children regard the dog, who again has fallen silent as he watches them with confused curiosity.

"You can't," Caleb says, in response to the palpable wave of need he feels emanating from the children. "You just can't."

Headless, The Mother. Around the yard at her feet are fragments of pumpkin, still sizzling from the heat of the shot. She turns her body to face him. She stays like that for quite some time, the children similarly silent and immobile at her side. Pain flaring in his knees, Caleb lowers himself back down into the chair. He feels no victory despite having fended them off for another year. He feels nothing but emptiness.

"You can't take Rufus," he mutters, and when next he looks up, the fragments of pumpkin are still in the dirt, the smell of burnt pumpkin in the air, but the visitors are gone.

Exhausted, drained, dispirited, Caleb sags in his chair, lets the shotgun clatter to the porch. Occasionally he helps himself to some candy from the pail but finds he can't taste it.

Later, as if sensing his sadness, Rufus comes and leaps up onto his lap, circling once as dogs do, before settling down, his head resting on his paws. Soon he is asleep. As Caleb strokes the dog's head, he looks out at the cornfield. The crickets are singing now, the moon returned from behind the clouds, bathing the field in silvery light. There is nothing to see out there. There won't be for another year, assuming he lives to see another Halloween. He hates to think what will happen if he doesn't.

"They can't have you," he whispers to the dog, and to the breeze. "Not yet."

He lights a cigarette and leans his head back to look at what few stars are there to be seen.

It is a promise he aims to keep. They can't take the only pure memory he has left, the only reason he has left to keep going.

At least until he is done with it, or until *it* is done with *him*.

Only then will he let them take what they so desperately need to make their family complete.

# RECOMMENDED BOOKS

Here are just a select few titles from my personal library—only a few of them Halloween-related in theme—that I recommend for a good, old-fashioned scare during the witching season. Please note, I'm sure there are a ferocious amount of books I love that are missing from this selection, and they're missing, not because I didn't want to include them, but because they were absent from the shelves I perused in order to compose this list. So please don't assume because a particular book is not here that I didn't enjoy it or deem it worthy. If I included every relevant book I've ever enjoyed, it would have taken me months, gone on for a hundred pages, and I'd *still* have missed some of them. So, this is just a shortlist of titles I recommend.

*The Last Days of Jack Sparks* by Jason Arnopp
*Broken Monsters* by Lauren Beukes
*Something Wicked this Way Comes* by Ray Bradbury
*Wuthering Heights* by Emily Brontë
*Ghosts of Yesterday* by Jack Cady
*The Hauntings of Hood Canal* by Jack Cady
*Heartsick* by Chelsea Cain
*Alone with the Horrors* by Ramsey Campbell
*October Dreams*, edited by Richard Chizmar
*October Dreams II*, edited by Richard Chizmar
*Trick R' Treat*, edited by Richard Chizmar
*Halloween Man* by Douglas Clegg
*Night Music* by John Connolly
*Nocturnes* by John Connolly
*The Whisperers* by John Connolly

*The Good House* by Tananarive Due

*Cutting Edge*, edited by Dennis Etchison

*Metahorror*, edited by Dennis Etchison

*Experimental Film* by Gemma Files

*Invasion of the Body Snatchers* by Jack Finney

*Sharp Objects* by Gillian Flynn

*Rune* by Christopher Fowler

*Spanky* by Christopher Fowler

*Smoke & Mirrors* by Neil Gaiman

*The Yellow Wallpaper and Other Writings* by Charlotte Perkins Gilman

*The Boys are Back in Town* by Christopher Golden

*Nightmare Seasons* by Charles L. Grant

*Raven* by Charles L. Grant

*Something Stirs* by Charles L. Grant

*The Black Carousel* by Charles L. Grant

*The Orchard*, by Charles L. Grant

*The Pet* by Charles L. Grant

*Into the Drowning Deep* by Mira Grant

*Four Octobers* by Rick Hautala

*My Best Friend's Exorcism* by Grady Hendrix

*Haunted* by James Herbert

*The Fog* by James Herbert

*The Ghosts of Sleath* by James Herbert

*The Rats* by James Herbert

*20th Century Ghosts* by Joe Hill

*Heart-Shaped Box* by Joe Hill

*NOS4A2* by Joe Hill

*The Woman in Black* by Susan Hill

*The Snowman's Children* by Glen Hirshberg

*The Two Sams: Ghost Stories* by Glen Hirshberg

*The Haunting of Hill House* by Shirley Jackson

*The Lottery and Other Stories* by Shirley Jackson

*The Grip of It* by Jac Jemc

*Mongrels* by Stephen Graham Jones

*The Silent Land* by Graham Joyce

*The Tooth Fairy* by Graham Joyce
*The Hunger* by Alma Katsu
*Providence* by Caroline Kepnes
*You* by Caroline Kepnes
*Peaceable Kingdom* by Jack Ketchum
*Red* by Jack Ketchum
*It* by Stephen King
*Full Dark, No Stars* by Stephen King
*Pet Sematary* by Stephen King
*Salem's Lot* by Stephen King
*The Shining* by Stephen King
*Dark Gods* by T.E.D. Klein
*The Ceremonies* by T.E.D. Klein
*The Cipher* by Kathe Koja
*Midnight* by Dean Koontz
*Odd Thomas* by Dean Koontz
*Phantoms* by Dean Koontz
*Conference with the Dead* by Terry Lamsley
*The Fisherman* by John Langan
*The Keeper* by Sarah Langan
*The Missing* by Sarah Langan
*High Cotton* by Joe R. Lansdale
*The Bottoms* by Joe R. Lansdale
*The Changeling* by Victor LaValle
*Macabre* by Stephen Laws
*Spectre* by Stephen Laws
*The Frighteners* by Stephen Laws
*Face* by Tim Lebbon
*The Nature of Balance* by Tim Lebbon
*White & Other Tales of Ruin* by Tim Lebbon
*Conjure Wife* by Fritz Leiber
*Our Lady of Darkness* by Fritz Leiber
*Rosemary's Baby* by Ira Levin
*The Stepford Wives* by Ira Levin
*The Nightmare Factory* by Thomas Ligotti

*Teatro Grottesco* by Thomas Ligotti
*The Shadow at the Bottom of the World* by Thomas Ligotti
*The Collection* by Bentley Little
*The Ignored* by Bentley Little
*The Policy* by Bentley Little
*The Resort* by Bentley Little
*Bone White* by Ronald Malfi
*Fevre Dream* by George R.R. Martin
*Burial* by Graham Masterton
*The Devil in Gray* by Graham Masterton
*Trauma* by Graham Masterton
*Hell House* by Richard Matheson
*I Am Legend* by Richard Matheson
*Blue World* by Robert R. McCammon
*The Listener* by Robert R. McCammon
*Mystery Walk* by Robert R. McCammon
*The Wolf's Hour* by Robert R. McCammon
*Dark Forces*, edited by Kirby McCauley
*Stitch* by Mark Morris
*Beloved* by Toni Morrison
*The Returned* by Jason Mott
*Dark Harvest* by Norman Partridge
*Johnny Halloween* by Norman Partridge
*Night Film* by Marisha Pessl
*The Family Plot* by Cherie Priest
*I'm Thinking of Ending Things* by Iain Reid
*Interview with the Vampire* by Anne Rice
*The Vampire Lestat* by Anne Rice
*Toybox* by Al Sarrantonio
*Hornets & Others* by Al Sarrantonio
*999*, edited by Al Sarrantonio
*The House Next Door* by Anne Rivers Siddons
*Chasing the Dead* by Joe Schreiber
*Song of Kali* by Dan Simmons
*Summer of Night* by Dan Simmons

*The Terror* by Dan Simmons
*More Tomorrow & Other Stories* by Michael Marshall Smith
*The Straw Men* by Michael Marshall Smith
*The Ruins* by Scott Smith
*Ghost Story* by Peter Straub
*At the Far Side of the Lake* by Steve Rasnic Tem
*City Fishing* by Steve Rasnic Tem
*The Other* by Thomas Tryon
*Why Not You & I?* by Karl Edward Wagner
*Sing, Unburied, Sing* by Jesmyn Ward
*Prime Evil*, edited by Douglas E Winter
*Figures in Rain* by Chet Williamson
*Soft & Others* by F. Paul Wilson

# RECOMMENDED MOVIES

This is not meant to be a list of the best horror movies of all time, though many of them certainly qualify, though it could also be argued that some of them aren't even *good* movies. Still, I think all serve perfectly as candidates for Halloween viewing. I, certainly, have fond memories of the occasions in which I was first exposed to them, so sentimentality plays a part. I'm sure there are quite a few I've forgotten, and even more that will leave you baffled as to why they were included in the first place, but hey, that's half the fun of lists, isn't it? The question is, how many have *you* seen?

*28 Days Later* (2002)
*28 Weeks Later* (2007)
*30 Days of Night* (2007)
*Absentia* (2011)
*A Girl Walks Home Alone at Night* (2014)
*A Nightmare on Elm Street* (1984)
*A Quiet Place* (2018)
*A Tale of Two Sisters* (2003)
*Alien* (1979)
*Aliens* (1986)
*Antichrist* (2009)
*An American Werewolf in London* (1981)
*Apollo 18* (2011)
*Backcountry* (2014)
*Battle Royale* (2000)
*Below* (2002)
*Black Death* (2010)
*Black Swan* (2010)

*Body Bags* (1993)
*Candyman* (1992)
*Carrie* (1976)
*Cat People* (1942)
*Child's Play* (1988)
*Clown* (2014)
*Creep* (2014)
*Creep 2* (2017)
*Creepshow* (1982)
*Creepshow II* (1987)
*Dark Night of the Scarecrow* (1981)
*Dark Skies* (2013)
*Dark Touch* (2013)
*Dawn of the Dead* (2004)
*Dead Alive* (1992)
*Dead Birds* (2004)
*Dead & Buried* (1981)
*Dead End* (2003)
*Dead Ringers* (1988)
*Dead Silence* (2007)
*Dead Snow* (2014)
*Devil's Pass* (2013)
*Dog Soldiers* (2002)
*Don't Breathe* (2016)
*Don't Look Now* (1973)
*Drag Me to Hell* (2009)
*Dread* (2009)
*Ed Wood* (1994)
*Europa Report* (2013)
*Event Horizon* (1997)
*Evil Dead* (2013)
*Evil Dead II* (1987)
*Final Destination* (2001)
*Final Destination 2* (2003)
*Final Destination 5* (2011)

*Flatliners* (1990)
*Frailty* (2001)
*Friday the 13th* (1980)
*Fright Night* (1985)
*Frozen* (2010)
*Gerald's Game* (2017)
*Get Out* (2017)
*Ghost Ship* (2002)
*Ginger Snaps* (2000)
*Goodnight Mommy* (2014)
*Grabbers* (2012)
*Grace* (2009)
*Grave Encounters* (2012)
*Green Room* (2015)
*Grim Prairie Tales* (1990)
*Halloween* (1978)
*Halloween II* (1981)
*Halloween H20* (1998)
*Halloween III: Season of the Witch* (1982)
*Happy Death Day* (2017)
*Hellraiser* (1987)
*Hereditary* (2018)
*High Tension* (2003)
*Honeymoon* (2014)
*House of the Devil* (2009)
*I Am the Pretty Thing That Lives in the House* (2016)
*I Saw the Devil* (2010)
*Ils (Them)* (2006)
*Inside* (2007)
*Insidious* (2011)
*In the Mouth of Madness* (1990)
*Invasion of the Body Snatchers* (1956)
*Invasion of the Body Snatchers* (1978)
*It* (2017)
*It Follows* (2014)

*Jacob's Ladder* (1990)
*Ju-On (The Grudge)* (2002)
*Kairo (Pulse)* (2001)
*Lake Mungo* (2008)
*Last Shift* (2014)
*Legion: Exorcist III* (1990)
*Let the Right One In* (2008)
*Lights Out* (2016)
*Lovely Molly* (2011)
*Martyrs* (2008)
*mother!* (2017)
*Mulberry Street* (2006)
*My Little Eye* (2002)
*Near Dark* (1987)
*Night of the Creeps* (1986)
*Night of the Demon* (1957)
*Night of the Living Dead* (1968)
*Oculus* (2013)
*Orphan* (2009)
*Paranormal Activity* (2007)
*Paranormal Activity 2* (2010)
*Possession* (1981)
*Predators* (2010)
*Prince of Darkness* (1990)
*Psycho* (1960)
*Pyewacket* (2017)
*Quarantine* (2008)
*R-Point* (2004)
*Re-animator* (1985)
*Return of the Living Dead* (1985)
*Rosemary's Baby* (1968)
*Scream* (1996)
*Session 9* (2001)
*Shaun of the Dead* (2004)
*Sinister* (2012)

*Sleep Tight* (2011)

*Sleepy Hollow* (1999)

*Slither* (2006)

*Something Wicked This Way Comes* (1983)

*Splinter* (2008)

*Split* (2016)

*Stake Land* (2010)

*Starry Eyes* (2014)

*Tales from the Crypt: Demon Knight* (1995)

*Tales from the Darkside: The Movie* (1990)

*Triangle* (2009)

*Trick R' Treat* (2009)

*Twilight Zone: The Movie* (1983)

*The Awakening* (2011)

*The Babadook* (2014)

*The Banshee Chapter* (2013)

*The Bay* (2012)

*The Blackcoat's Daughter* (2015)

*The Blair Witch Project* (1999)

*The Body Snatcher* (1945)

*The Brood* (1979)

*The Cabin in the Woods* (2011)

*The Canal* (2014)

*The Changeling* (1980)

*The Collector* (2009)

*The Collection* (2012)

*The Company of Wolves* (1984)

*The Conjuring* (2013)

*The Conspiracy* (2012)

*The Crazies* (2010)

*The Crow* (1994)

*The Descent* (2005)

*The Devil's Backbone* (2001)

*The Eclipse* (2009)

*The Endless* (2017)

*The Exorcism of Emily Rose* (2005)
*The Exorcist* (1973)
*The Eye* (2002)
*The Eye 2* (2004)
*The Eyes of My Mother* (2016)
*The Fly* (1986)
*The Fog* (1981)
*The Gate* (1987)
*The Hallow* (2015)
*The Haunting* (1963)
*The Howling* (1981)
*The Innocents* (1961)
*The Invitation* (2015)
*The Loved Ones* (2009)
*The Mist* (2007)
*The Mothman Prophecies* (2002)
*The Omen* (1976)
*The Omen II* (1978)
*The Orphanage* (2007)
*The Others* (2001)
*The Pact* (2012)
*The Possession* (2012)
*The Reef* (2010)
*The Ring* (2002)
*The Ritual* (2017)
*The Shining* (1980)
*The Shrine* (2010)
*The Sixth Sense* (1999)
*The Strangers* (2008)
*The Taking of Deborah Logan* (2014)
*The Texas Chainsaw Massacre* (1974)
*The Thaw* (2009)
*The Thing* (1982)
*The Visit* (2015)
*The Wicker Man* (1973)

*The Witch* (2015)
*The Woods* (2006)
*They* (2002)
*They Look Like People* (2015)
*Thirst* (2009)
*Troll Hunter* (2010)
*Tucker and Dale Vs Evil* (2010)
*Under the Shadow* (2016)
*Unfriended* (2014)
*Vanishing on 7th Street* (2010)
*V/H/S/2* (2013)
*We Are Still Here* (2015)
*Wind Chill* (2007)
*Willow Creek* (2013)
*Zombieland* (2009)

# ABOUT THE AUTHOR

Born and raised in a small harbor town in the south of Ireland, Kealan Patrick Burke knew from a very early age that he was going to be a horror writer. The combination of an ancient locale, a horror-loving mother, and a family full of storytellers, made it inevitable that he would end up telling stories for a living. Since those formative years, he has written five novels, over a hundred short stories, six collections, and edited four acclaimed anthologies. In 2004, he was honored with the Bram Stoker Award for his novella *The Turtle Boy*.

Kealan has worked as a waiter, a drama teacher, a mapmaker, a security guard, an assembly-line worker at Apple Computers, a salesman (for a day), a bartender, landscape gardener, vocalist in a grunge band, curriculum content editor, fiction editor at Gothic.net, and, most recently, a fraud investigator.

When not writing, Kealan designs book covers through his company Elderlemon Design.

Several of his books have been optioned for film.

Visit him on the web at www.kealanpatrickburke.com

Printed in Great Britain
by Amazon

62162047R00078